LOVE is not always *EASY*

LOVE is not always *EASY*

James Earl Jackson

1603 Capitol Ave., Suite 310 Cheyenne, Wyoming USA 82001
1-888-980-6523 | admin@urlinkpublishing.com

URLink Print and Media is committed to excellence in the publishing industry.

Book design copyright © 2021 by URLink Print and Media. All rights reserved.

Published in the United States of America

Library of Congress Control Number: 2021917951
ISBN 978-1-64753-934-4 (Paperback)
ISBN 978-1-64753-935-1 (Hardback)
ISBN 978-1-64753-936-8 (Digital)

26.05.21

CHAPTER

1

It is an early Tuesday afternoon with overcast conditions, chilly temperatures, and a steady stream of rain, just enough to make for miserable conditions. James Lackey, a fifty-eight-year-old man, sits at the graveyard staring at the casket that holds the body of his wife Margie of thirty-four years. Sitting next to James on each side are their two daughters Pam Mills and Debbie Samuels. Margie and James were high school sweethearts and had always been a couple. They met first in elementary school, had their first date in high school, and had been together every since except for the time James was drafted into the US Army where he spent his tour of duty, serving his country with the US Army's 101st Airborne Division, which included a tour of duty in Vietnam.

Pam, thirty-one, and Debbie, twenty-eight, are both married and parents of two children each. Pam is married to Joe Mills Sr. They have a son, Joe Jr., seven, and a daughter, Regina, five years old. Debbie is married to Frank Samuels, employed as a middle management executive in a major corporation; they are the parents of Lauren, four, and Christina, two years old. Debbie is known in the family as the aggressive daughter, very feisty, while Pam is a bit more

5

reserved. Her husband is an attorney employed at the same firm as her dad, James Lackey, who is a Senior partner with the firm.

The minister, Pastor Arnold Bledsoe, a very charismatic personality and lifelong friend to James Lackey, delivers the graveside message as members of the family is emotional and is displaying their emotions mostly in a quiet tone. The pastor does not want to prolong the services due to the weather condition and is trying to not appear as if though he is rushing his message but presenting it with taste. Upon the conclusion of the services, teary-eyed James extends his hands to Pam, Debbie, Joe, Frank, and all four of the grandchildren. He thanks his friend Pastor Bledsoe and hugs his family.

Sam Lackey, James's older brother, and Mary Chambers, his sister, walk over to join James and his family. They all embrace each other as a family. Mary whispers to James, "We love you very much. We love this family and will be there for all of you." Emotions are reserved as the host of family members and friends begin to exit from the cemetery and head for the home of Margie and James Lackey, where food and drinks are being served, hoping for a more pleasant atmosphere, maybe a few smiles, maybe even a bit of laughter.

Everyone is thinking that only if Margie could speak to them now, her words at a time like this would probably be, "There is a time for sadness and there is this time, so let us all look happy, cheer up, and smile. Tomorrow will be here no matter how we feel."

James and his family enter the limousine for the ride home. All of the adults are very quite except the kids who are playing with each other and asking questions about where will their grandmother be. Joe Jr., the oldest of the kids in the limo, is trying to be the adult of the kids and acts the part by explaining everything to the younger children. James, thinking about all of the loneliness in his future, talks to his grandchildren by telling them that their grandmother will now be in a safe and sacred place.

After a ride through the streets and the entrance into the neighborhood that James and Margie have shared for so many years, the limo finally arrives at their home. The family exits to find out that many of their family and friends that attended the funeral services have arrived at the house already and are circulating throughout the house waiting for James and his family, everyone greets them. James is not feeling particularly cheerful as of the moment but knows that it is his place to create a joyous and friendly mood. James quickly speaks up, by thanking everyone for being with him and his family during these trying times, and asks his lifelong friend, Pastor Arnold Bledsoe, to bless the food and to say a prayer for everyone and give thanks to God. Pastor Bledsoe speaks as James requested and is thanking everyone for being there for his friend. He asks God for his continued blessings in the house. The pastor concludes the very short prayer. James announces, "I see we have a lot of wonderful-looking food. It smells good, and my"—sampling a taste of food—"it also taste good. Let's eat all of this food that is here. If we need more, there is plenty more that we will get."

"Debbie here"—placing his arm around her shoulder—"is in charge of making sure there is enough food and drinks for you. Let's have a good time. Just enjoy yourself because that is what Margie would have wanted."

James's older brother Sam made his way over to James to embrace him and to say, "God bless you, my little brother, and may God be with you in these trying times." Sam asks

James if he has any immediate plans to relax before going back to work.

James responds with, "I have not even thought about anything yet, even though this has not been anything sudden. It is not what I wanted to admit and plan for."

"I understand. Remember, I am here when you need a shoulder to cry on or an ear to listen. I will always be here." James thanks his brother and, quietly trying not to be noticed, makes his way to the bedroom for some alone time. He is not in a joyous mood and does not want to spoil the celebration for his guest. The house is a little overcrowded, but festive. Everyone seems to be enjoying themselves. People are renewing old friendships and, in some instances, meeting and greeting for the first time. They are enjoying all of the good food and drinks being served. Debbie soon notices that her dad is not present. Thinking that he must be miserable, she approaches her sister Pam and asks if she knows where their dad has disappeared to.

Pam says, "I believe he is upstairs in his bedroom. At least I have seen him heading in that direction. I decided to let him be alone. He needs some alone time now. Life is not going to be much fun for him anytime soon. You and I will have to be there."

"I know things are going to be difficult for Daddy and he will definitely need our support going forward, but I am still going up to be with him and see if he needs anything. I will be up with him for a while to let him know that I am here right now."

"I guess we can at least go up and let him know that we understand what he is going through and that he is not alone."

Pam nods toward her Aunt Mary and suggests that Aunt Mary is in charge as she explains to Aunt Mary what the two of them are about to do. "We also will miss our mother."

Debbie says, "Maybe that is a good idea. The both of us should pay a visit to Mom and Dad's room." The girls enter their dad's bedroom and notices him sitting on the bed crying. The two of them sits next to their dad and puts their arm around him and tells him that they understand and miss their mom. They will be a strong family and pull through this together because that is what their mom would have wanted.

James says, "I did not want you girls to see me like this." Pam and Debbie embrace their dad with a few tears of their own.

"Let's all have a cry together."

—m—

The strain on James Lackey and his daughters becomes much more visible as they are now all alone in James and Margie's bedroom without Margie and the host of friends and relatives that has been visiting with them since their loss of Margie.

Pam says, "I am not happy. Mom won't be back no more, and I miss her so much. I won't have her shoulder to cry on anymore. I know if she could talk to me now, she would explain to me that my life must continue. She would remind me that I have a wonderful husband that loves me very much and two great kids that make me proud to be a mommy."

James hugs both daughters and says, "Even though our most precious Margie has moved on to enjoy her ultimate reward, which is eternal life in heaven with God, she would want the three of us to continue with our lives, and one day if we prepare ourselves well, we can join her and also be embraced by Jesus in a much better place."

Debbie says, "I miss my mommy too, but I promised her that I will carry on. I will miss her embrace. I will miss the advice from her that I always pretended not to listen to. I will miss coming over to the house and hearing her say, 'You better eat something. I know you are hungry.' I will miss her telling me that I never listen. Mom, I am listening. I have always listened to everything you have told me. I just pretended not to listen."

James hugs Debbie a little closer as she becomes emotional and says, "Mommy hears you, baby doll. We all miss her, and we are going to go on just as Mommy would want us to."

All three of them are now crying when Pam says, "We are going to have to be adults about our loss. We cannot let Mom down."

James says as the crying continues, "We just had to get this out of our system. We are going to continue with our lives."

After a period of time passes while upstairs with their dad, Pam and Debbie are thinking that their guest must be feeling neglected and return to the downstairs area, where they find their Aunt Mary being a wonderful host. Soon, James feels composed enough to make his way back downstairs to mingle with the guests and to thank them for being so supportive. James's brother Sam approaches James to tell him that he wants a private moment with him. Sam told James that he has taken a few extra days of from the business, and that his son Grant could run things until he returns. Sam tells James that he would like for James to join him on a short trip to Hawaii to just spend some time relaxing on the beach and playing a little golf, and putting their minds at ease.

James thanks his brother but tells Sam that his place is there at home, being that he has missed so many days away from the office during Margie's illness that he has a lot of catching up to do. Sam tell James, "I checked with your office. Everybody tells me that you should take a little time off. You are covered until whenever you decide to return to work. After all, you are the boss, unless you forgot."

James answers, "You know I have to set the example and be there!"

"Well, little brother, don't say I didn't try. The offer will remain on the table if you change your mind. You know where to find me."

"Thanks, brother, I do know where to find you."

At which time, James and Sam's sister Mary approaches her two brothers and asks them, "Are you keeping secrets from me. Remember, I am a part of this family too, and you must not forget that I am also Daddy's favorite."

Sam says, "Sis, I was trying to invite James on a little getaway trip to put his mind at ease."

Mary looking at James inquires, "Well!"

James says, "I have to get back to the office. I have missed too much time lately."

Mary argues, "Brother, that work will be there whenever you get back."

"That is what I told him."

"Thanks to both of you for your concern, but I had better stop ignoring the guest. I know both of you have my best interest at heart, and if I change my mind, I will let both of you know, but right now, I had better start mingling with the guests." James, Sam, and Mary smile at each other and respect each other's view as they start to mingle with the guests again.

—⚏—

Later that week, James has spent most of his time grieving the loss of his wife. At times, James feels as if though he does not want to socialize with friends or family, and other times, James feels that maybe he should have taken his brother Sam up on his offer to take that trip to Hawaii to play a little golf. James has returned to work instead, even though his mind is not on work. James is not accomplishing very much, mostly complicating matters for everyone else around the office. James is bitter at Margie for not being there with him and does not feel justified for feeling that way because Margie has suffered a great deal with her illness. Being bitter at Margie and rude to the office staff are totally uncalled for, but James is miserable and lonely.

James decides to leave the office early and informs Mary that he is leaving early but does not tell her where he is going or if he should be contacted. James has no plans to do anything, so he decides to just drive around. James is now driving with his music playing loud in the car. First stop is his home golf course where he decides to hit a few golf balls. Soon this is not much fun, so he once again finds himself driving over a hundred miles completely out of the city and is now driving the interstate highway. James soon has to stop for gas. He stops at a large truck stop where truckers purchase gas and eat. James fills up his car with gas and realizes that he is now hungry after seeing the truck stop diner that caters to truckers. James enters the diner and is told to sit wherever he can find a seat. James soon finds a seat and is issued a menu. As he is deciding on what to order, a woman truck drivers asked him if it is all right that she sit with him because it is the only seat she can find. James tells her that he would be happy if she would join him. James stands and helps her as she sits and introduces himself to her. She introduces herself as Joan. James asks her if she is driving one of those big rigs outside.

Joan says, "Yes, I am afraid so. I have to make a living."

James replies, "Are you one of those truckers that drive on long trips with heavy loads?"

"Well occasionally, I am on the road for days at a time. I am a single mom with two growing teenage boys that eat a lot."

"Do the boys get much quality time with you?"

Joan, smiling, answers, "You ask a lot of questions."

"I am sorry. That is very rude of me."

"That is okay. You see, my mother and father take care of the boys when I am on the road. Sometimes, the boys travel with me when they are not in school." The server is at the table to take their order.

Joan says, "I will have my usual. The cheeseburger with fries and a large coke." James orders soup and a half sandwich. James asks the server if the lemonade is concentrated. The server says it is concentrated.

James says, "Bring me ice tea." The server finishes their order and departs.

James resumes the conversation with Joan. "I admire you for all the sacrifices and effort that it must take to raise two boys. I have two girls that I had a lot of help raising. They are now all grown up. Each of the girls are married with two kids each. I now live alone. I recently lost my wife to breast cancer, so forgive me if I am not a lot of fun."

"I can understand your pain. My late husband was killed by someone trying to rob him a little over six years ago. This left me with two boys and a job that was not paying me much of a salary. I had to find a job that pays enough to take care of my two boys, so now I am a truck driver."

"Well I guess we both understand the difficulty of losing a loved one."

"I don't believe you are a truck driver, dressed the way you are dressed. Your suit is designer and expensive. What do you do for a living?"

"I am a partner in a law firm. I am a lawyer. I was lonely today, mourning the loss of my wife. I left the office earlier today and started driving, and before I knew it, I was over a hundred miles out of the city, in need of gas. I stopped here for gas and decided to try the food in this diner."

"I am sure you have had better."

"The food does not look that bad. Now if it only tastes as good as it looks."

"Well truck stop food is not fancy but it taste good. Either it tastes good or I am always hungry when I eat and don't realize it is lousy."

The server arrives with the food. James and Joan begin to eat their food. James looks at Joan and says, "So far so good. How is your cheeseburger?"

Joan answers, "I always eat cheeseburgers when I stop here."

"You must drive this way a lot."

"This is one of my regular routes."

The two of them soon finishes their food and Joan tells James, "It was a pleasure sitting with you. I must hit the road. I am on a schedule."

"I will take your check."

"That is okay. I got it."

"You take care of those boys and drive safely. Let me have your check."

Joan, a little hesitant, says as she leaves, "Well thank you. It really has been pleasant for me also."

James says bye to Joan as he prepares to pay the checks. James soon leaves.

—∞—

It is now time for James to take the long drive back home. The music is again playing. Only this time, it is much louder and the drive seems much longer. It seems that there are many more trucks traveling the highway. James soon finds himself sleepy and tired, so he figures that it will not be safe to continue driving when he observes a public rest stop. James decides to stop at this rest stop to maybe rest long enough to wake up and drive safely. He finally locates a comfortable place to park and takes a nap. James locks all of the doors to his automobile, lets his seat back to rest, and quickly falls asleep. James is awakened shortly by a person that seems to be homeless, knocking on his window and asking James if he has any spare change. James is wondering how this person is at this highway rest stop without a car. James lets the window down and starts conversation with this person by asking him where he is parked. This person identifies himself as Joe and points toward an old van that he tells James is his means of transportation. James exits his car to take a walk over to Joe's van where he observes that this van is loaded down with all of Joe's possessions that looks mostly like junk.

James asks him where is he headed, and his response is, "I have no destination in mind. I will probably end up wherever the gas that I can purchase with the money that people like you will give me. I hope Hollywood."

James asks, "What about food?"

Joe responds, "I don't have any money for food."

"Man, how in the world did you end up out here broke, with no food?"

"Well I started out in Chicago about two months ago, and this is as far I have gotten. I am hoping to end up eventually in Hollywood and when I become one of those movie actors. When I clean myself up, I am not a bad-looking dude. I was working back in the Chicago area, just outside of Chicago. I got laid off from my job. I looked around for awhile for work with no success, so about two months ago, I got into my van and headed west. My goal is Hollywood. I am stranded here until I can get enough money to continue my trip."

James asks Joe, "Are you hungry?"

"Yep!"

James, feeling a bit generous, pulls out some money and hands it to Joe. "I hope this will help."

Joe looks at the money and says, "This will help a lot, man, thank you. I can eat, buy some gas, and get a good night's rest. I just might be able to make it all the way to Hollywood now. Where can I get in touch with you, so when I become big Hollywood star, I can pay you back?"

"Well, man, you don't have to pay me back, but here is my card in case you ever need a lawyer when you become a big star."

Joe shakes Jame's hand and says, "Man, I really want to thank you," and rushes of to his van.

James is not feeling sleepy anymore and decides to once again head for home. James has not thought about Margie for a few hours now, turns up the music, and begins the drive home, thinking just how eventful this day has been.

—◊◊—

Few months pass, James's grief for Margie continues and is now becoming more and more consumed with grandkids and work at the office. Even though his mind is not into his

16

work, he seems bitter at Margie for leaving him. Finally one day, Debbie decides to drop by the office to pay his dad a visit and invite him out to lunch. James accepts Debbie's lunch invitation and joins her for lunch. During their lunch date, Debbie requests that James try and cheer himself up by doing something special, maybe take some time off from work, take a trip somewhere, take a cruise, get together with family, or have an outing with the family maybe at a favorite family restaurant for dinner.

James says, Maybe I would like having dinner with my family."

"Like what?"

"A dinner with the family."

"You want to have a family dinner?"

"Yes, I think having dinner with my family is a wonderful idea."

Debbie is a little shocked that her dad has accepted a dinner date with his family. "Well a get-together dinner with the family it is. Let me call Pam and Joe, Aunt Mary, and Aunt Carol to set a date and time, which I hope will be this weekend. I will get back with you with the information. I am going to make the reservation at your and Mom's favorite restaurant."

"Make the reservation wherever you guys feel comfortable. I will be happy to get together with my family."

"Just leave everything to me." James and Debbie continue their lunch.

—⚬⚬—

While continuing his grief in his office later that afternoon long after the departure of Debbie, Mary rings James that he has a phone call from a young lady by the name of Joan.

"Did she tell you the purpose of her call?"

"She tells me that you might not remember her, but she met you at a truck stop a few months back."

James suddenly remembers and says, "I will speak with her." James answers the phone. "James Lackey, may I help you?"

Joan replies, "You might not remember me, but I met you a few months ago at a truck stop. I asked if it would be okay if I sit with you because there were no vacant tables."

"I do remember you as the single mom raising two boys."

"Yes, that is me. It just so happens that I am in this fair city to make a drop off and decided to call you to once again say thanks for being so kind to me that night. I was a little bit depressed and you lifted my spirits."

"I think I remember telling you that I would not be a fun person that night."

"I do remember you telling me that you were mourning the loss of your wife."

"I am still not much of a fun person."

"You should let someone else be the judge of where you measure on the fun scale. I enjoyed having dinner with you that night, and I wanted to let you know how much I appreciated your kindness."

"Thank you. That day and night ended as a pretty gratifying day and night for me also. If you are going to be around town for awhile, maybe we can have a bite and a drink."

"I am afraid I will have to take a rain check. I have my load and the highway is calling."

"Maybe your next trip!"

"I will call you," she says jokingly. "I found out that the number works. I also have your cell number on your card."

"You know how to get me. Until your next trip, I will say so long."

"So long." She hangs up and rushes off to get on the road.

—∞—

The dinner date and reservations are set. There had been concern by some members of the members of the family that maybe this favorite restaurant of James and Margie's past might not be such a good idea because after all, this also the restaurant that James and Margie enjoyed some of their most memorable outings. The decision is that the family would get together at the restaurant. After all, this is the restaurant that Margie and James have celebrated some of their most memorable occasions. The restaurant can also accommodate the family in a special room setup for large family gathering such as the Lackey family. James is happy with the restaurant selection that will rekindle a lot of fond memories and he is well known by the restaurant staff.

The day of the dinner has arrived, and the family arrives at the restaurant with long faces, just to show James what he has presented to them lately. The sad faces soon turn into smiles and happiness. After observing his family, James suddenly becomes lively, also remembering all of the times that he and Margie have enjoyed there. The family is soon seated in the private room that Debbie had requested and is presented with menus.

The family becomes engaged in family conversation and pays little attention to the menus that has been presented to them. After some time passes, the servers have served the table with bread and water for everyone. The server asks if anyone is ready to order their food. The family is having so much fun meeting and greeting each other that no one is ready to order and has not even read the menu.

Debbie suggests, "We had better decide what we are going to order." Finally, everyone is reading the menu and deciding what they are going to order. After everyone has finally decided what they are going to order and placed their order, the lively conversation has continued. After all has been served and the family has finished eating, they are waiting to place their desert orders.

James stands and addresses his family, thanking all of them for inviting him out. "Whoever came up with this idea really had a good one, and I needed this." The family is now joyous and takes their time before ordering desert, enjoying the moment with laughter and fun, by telling a few humorous family stories. Finally, the family begins to order their desert. James is suggesting deserts that he and Margie have always enjoyed in the pass, which most members of the family found to be to their liking as they placed their order. The dinner date is finally coming to an end. All is saying their good-byes and heading for home. James enters his car for the drive home feeling good and also feeling that the night has been a big success.

James is back at work, remembering the family's get-together, thinking that maybe they should do that more often. The family's outing is a very nice gesture. He hopes that it won't be so long before the next one, but James continues to spend his time not being in a very good mood and bitter at Margie. He continues his life with limited social activity. James also finds himself thinking about Joan, and maybe her contacting him could lead to maybe a social outlet. The two of them have a lot in common with each other, even though Joan is much younger than him. James is not interested in a romance. After all, Margie remains the love of James's life, just a little social time, an occasional dinner date when Joan is in town. Family members continue to remind James that he has to get his life back together, maybe a vacation.

His brother Sam reminds James of his offer that the two brothers get away, have a little fun, and does not have to be Hawaii, maybe they could go fishing or maybe James should start dating. James thinking, *Start dating? I wouldn't think of going out with another woman. Why should I take a vacation? Margie won't be there with me to enjoy. No, sir, my taking a vacation would not be fair to Margie. I am all right. Maybe a dinner date without the attachment of any romantic interest once in awhile with a much younger woman could be the answer.*

After much coursing by the entire family, James surprises his brother Sam and agrees to an occasional weekend golf with Sam and either James's two sons-in-laws or a couple of Sam's sons. And every once in a while when the time permits, Sam's daughter Patty joins their foursome. James has always enjoyed a round of golf with his brother Sam, and when Sam's daughter Patty plays with them, it is even more of a pleasant outing. Patty just so happens to be the family's best golfer and at one time flirted with a career on the LPGA but never quite made it. These occasional golf outings serves as stimulation of sort for James in that it makes for less time to dwell on the loss of Margie. Maybe these golf outings should happen more frequently. At least it is better than James being all alone with himself, with nothing to do. His entertainment with nothing to do always leads to some bar with strangers and having multiple drinks until closing time.

James's daughters are constantly worrying about James's activities or the lack there off. He is so unlike himself since their mom's passing. Debbie and Pam are always happiest when their dad is spending time with members of the family, especially their Uncle Sam. James and Sam have always been very close as brothers that have always enjoyed spending quality time together. All of James's adult life as far back as Pam and Debbie could remember, their father only had an occasional drink socially at dinner, or social events and maybe whenever their mom and dad were celebrating a life achievement of some sort. Pam and Debbie are constantly asking their dad the reason for his stranger-than-usual actions, and the answer to Pam and Debbie is always the same, he blames their mom for leaving him. "I will be all right. You guys go and enjoy the wonderful life you have. Take care of my grandkids."

Soon the social life of James Earl Lackey began to expand beyond a life of drinks at the neighborhood bar and an occasional golf outing with his brother Sam to celebrating a newfound social life drinking and involving himself with whatever woman that would make herself available to his needs. There was never a shortage of women. James met many women that he was not very proud of and would not even think of introducing to his precious family. Even though James's social life is at an all time low, he never forgets his family, especially those four grandchildren. James is always planning for the grandkids, always purchasing little souvenirs whenever he is out of town on a business trip, calling them every day. He just loves his grandchildren and feels that there is no greater honor in his life today then being a grandpa. His grandchildren love and adore him in return. James is seen spending time with his grandchildren in many ways. He watches cartoons with them, attends all school events that his grandkids are participating in, attends all of their little league sporting events, visits children amusement parks, and takes them to see the latest movies for kids, and they are always spending time at their grandpa's house on his days off. Even though James finds this much time for his grandchildren, he also has a new social life that he is not very proud of and knows that it is a life that his two daughters would scold him for or a life that he does not want to include any of his family, especially his grandkids.

Late one evening, James is at one of the locations that he has been spending much of his time at lately drinking and picking up his one-night-stand women. He is about to depart with his usual one night stand, a young woman that he met while sitting at the bar drinking, when a young man approaches him and asks James if he is trying to pick up on his woman. James not wanting to become involved in any kind of confrontation quickly tells the young man that he just met the woman and that they had only shared a couple of drinks. The young man tells James that the woman he has been sharing drinks with is his wife and they have two kids at home.

James says, "I just met her." At this time, James realizes that he does not even know this woman's name. The young man grabs the woman's arm and forcibly tells her that she going home. The woman pulls her arm away from the young man and tells him, "I am not going with you anywhere. You can go f—yourself. James realizes that the best thing for him to do is pay his bar tab and leave. He quickly tells the two of them that he is leaving. James quickly pays his bar tab and leaves the two of them involved in an intense argument. James is now in his car heading for home, shaking and frightened from the encounter, thinking about what could have happened and just what is his life turning into. James finally reaches home and is still frightened from his night's outing, realizing that he will not be returning to that establishment.

The following day, James is driving along the busy city streets of Los Angeles, California's Miracle Mile district, still thinking about the previous night's encounter. He is stuck in traffic, listening to the radio, when he hears the voice of his old friend Rev. Arnold Bledsoe, the charismatic pastor from the church that he and Margie hace attended from the first day that Pastor Bledsoe began his pastorship there. James has not been attending church very much lately, but hearing the pastor's voice has brought back many happy memories for James, memories if James and Margie attending church services and hearing Pastor Bledsoe's powerful Sunday morning messages. James now remembers all of the gratification that this church has provided for him and Margie. James decides that it is about time he returns to the church and have a conversation with his friend, Pastor Arnold Bledsoe. An illegal U-turn leads James in the direction of the church. Once he arrives at the church, James is a bit hesitant at first to enter, feeling guilty for not attending and participating in church services lately. He is not sure he really wants to unload all of his problems on his friend and also his pastor. He soon decides that it will be good to have a little talk with the his pastor, whom he has not seen lately. James completes his drive and exits his car to proceed to the office of Pastor Bledsoe, not knowing if the pastor would be in or not, but he is going to take a chance on his being there anyway. James arrives at the church and feels a little strange as he enters the unlocked doors. James immediately recognizes the pastor standing outside of his small office as if though he is expecting James.

Pastor Bledsoe with a great big smile says to James, "Welcome, my friend, I was wondering what has taken you so long. Make yourself comfortable in God's house."

James says, "Pastor, I guess it is the lonely state that my life is in right now. I need help!"

James and Pastor Bledsoe enter Pastor Bledsoe's office and proceed to have a wonderful conversation that lasts over an hour. James spent most of the time telling the pastor how his life has deteriorated to its current sate and how lost he feels without Margie being in his life. Pastor Bledsoe tells James, "God is with you. God knows your outcome. Worrying will not change what your outcome will be. You must be strong, don't be discouraged."

James replies, "I hear exactly what you are saying, Pastor. It has been difficult. Sometimes I feel that Margie just up and left me."

"You are now in God's house, don't be angry. Just have faith and trust in the Lord. Your life has much to offer. Margie did not just up and leave you. She left you in good hands. She left you with a wonderful family that loves you. You have a successful career. Come back and include God again to make your life complete. That is how Margie would want your life to continue, not moping around as an angry man."

James feeling much better now. He thanks the pastor and prepares to leave for home. "I will see you Sunday, Pastor. I want to thank you!"

—⁓—

It is now Sunday, and James is keeping his word to Pastor Bledsoe by attending church services. James feels very comfortable and feels that he has found his way back where he belongs. "Yes, It feels good this Sunday morning!" James is now finally once again attending church services just like the old time, and he is once again enjoying the church environment. James loves to take the grandkids with him mostly when they are not attending services with their parents. James loves it even more when either one or both of his daughters and their families attend church services with him. A few weeks later, James is very happy. Pam, Debbie, and both their families are attending church with James. During Pastor Bledsoe's sermon and announcements, he points out to the congregation just how much James's life has turned around since the lost of his wife. Most of the church members present remember Margie. Church services are over; Debbie and Pam are trying to speak with Pastor Bledsoe. After a brief period of time, the two of them are able to thank the pastor for all he has been doing to help their father with his struggles.

CHAPTER

2

A couple of years pass, James has been attending church service regularly, still lonely, but now he has a much more stable life. This Sunday morning while James is at church services, he notices a longtime member that he has seen many times at church, a Mrs. Claudette Maddox, making her way in his direction and finally she sits next to James. Claudette just so happens to be a widow also, with a very good reputation as an active church member that lost her husband a short time before James lost his wife Margie. James has never had a reason to develop a friendship or relationship with Mrs. Maddox, but this Sunday, Mrs. Maddox seems to have purposely made her way to direction of where James is sitting and has sat next to him. Mrs. Maddox starts a friendly conversation with James, by first introducing herself to James as if though James does not know her. James is a bit suspicious that maybe Mrs. Maddox has her reasons, and they could be a bit more than just being a fellow church member or asking to join some church organization. James decides that maybe he will make the conversation with her this day; it has been over two years since the death of Margie, and maybe a little friendly companionship with someone other than all of those pass relationships with those girls at those bars is just what is needed. James and Claudette start to chat in a whispering voice, but soon they begin to listen to the pastor's sermon. Immediately following the services, James and Claudette walk out of the church together and begin to engage in conversation. Claudette asks James, "Did you enjoy the sermon?"

James responds, "It was an on time service. I enjoyed it. Pastor Bledsoe is always right on time and truthful. I always enjoy his services. I just want to ask if you have plans this afternoon.

Claudette's response is, "None at all, just going home and watch a little TV." James asks Claudette to join him for a bite to eat at a neighborhood restaurant that many of the members of the church's congregation frequent on Sunday after church. Claudette arrive at the restaurant in separate cars and enter the restaurant to eat. They are seated in a booth immediately and begin talking where they soon find out that the two of them have much in common. The conversation is very enjoyable to both of them. The server has taken their order and has returned with their meal. James and Claudette continue their conversation as they eat. Finally the two of them finish their meal and agree that maybe it is not a bad idea for the two of them to see each other in the future.

James and Claudette's after-church-services meal leads to more outings that are not always after-church meals. Finally one day, after always having meals and dinners with James, Claudette is thinking, *Why not invite James over for one of my home-cooked meals?* And places a call to James at his office to pretend to just speak with him. During the conversation,

Claudette invites James over to her house for a home-cooked meal. James immediately accepts. James asks Claudette if she has any specific date and time in mind. Claudette tells James, "Why not tonight?"

James tells Claudette, "Tonight will be perfect."

"Maybe I should get off the phone and start preparing dinner."

"Well I guess that means that I will see you right after I leave the office."

"I will see you then."

James arrives at Claudette's home for dinner. This is James's first visit to Claudette's house, which is a somewhat large house located in an upscale neighborhood. Claudette has finished preparing the meal and has the table all set for two people in her dinning room. James tells Claudette that he would like to wash up before they start eating. Claudette points out to James the location of the bathroom. James enters the bathroom, and once he completes washing up, Claudette presents James a choice for a glass of wine. James decides on a glass of red wine and says, "I do not know if red wine is appropriate for our meal because I don't know what the menu is."

Claudette, smiling, says, "Red wine is the correct one."

"I have a taste for this red one anyway." After a bit more conversation, James and Claudette decide that it is time that they begin eating. James is impressed with the meal and realizes that Claudette is a really good cook and tells Claudette that the food is very tasty and not allow him to make a pig out of himself.

Claudette replies, "Just enjoy. I don't have much reason to cook these days unless some or all of my adult children and their family notify me that they will have a meal with me.

My youngest son Brad stops by to raid the refrigerator fairly regular." James and Claudette continue their meal. Soon the meal and desert have all been served and is over.

James tells Claudette that he has enjoyed the meal and is also enjoying his time with her. Claudette thanks James for the compliments and tells James that being with him is also enjoyable. Claudette tells James that she has had her sights on him for sometime now. James smiles and tells Claudette that he has noticed her for some time but did not think it would be appropriate for him to approach her, so he just kept his mouth shut, but he is glad that Claudette chooses him to sit with that Sunday.

As time passes, James and Claudette are beginning to spend lots of time together. Neither of them is telling their families that they are spending time together. Soon it becomes obvious to Pastor Bledsoe and the church congregation that James and Claudette are now a couple. James and Claudette begin to attend church together as a couple. James and Claudette are together at Claudette's house discussing the possibilities of making their relationship known to their family and how it will be received.

Claudette remarks, "I don't know how our relationship will be received by my adult children."

James answers, "I am pretty sure my youngest daughter will not be receptive to my having a relationship with another woman, but my oldest daughter probably will be happy for me."

"Well you know we are going to have to tell them soon."

"Real soon."

"I am sure my daughter will be happy for me. She has often mentioned to me that I need to get a life. She feels that her mom is in need of companionship with a nice respectable man my age."

James, laughing, says, "Have you found that nice respectable man your age?"

Claudette, smiling, teased, "Maybe."

—⦵—

Meanwhile, James's daughters Pam and Debbie are engaged in conversation on the telephone, expressing their suspicions that something is going on in their father's life that he is not telling them about, realizing for some time now that they are not seeing their father that often. He must have other interest, because he does not call either of them or the kids much anymore or to spend time with the kids or the two of them. The kids miss their grandfather and have been asking questions like, "Where is Grandpa?" or "Is Grandpa all right?" Pam and Debbie begin to wonder what is new in their father's life. Maybe he has reverted to drinking and seeing all of those loose women again. If that is true, they will not like his life.

Debbie says, "We have not attended church with Daddy lately. Maybe if we surprised him at church on Sunday to see if he still attending church, we could then get some idea of what is going on in his life.Maybe he will take us to that little eatery that he and Mom used to frequent after church services for lunch." Debbie and Pam both decide that maybe the two of them and their families should surprise their dad this coming Sunday morning by joining him in church services, but after remembering that two of them already have commitments for Sunday at their church, maybe they will have to surprise their daddy another day.

—⦵—

James and Claudette are once again at the home of Claudette. She is once again preparing dinner for her and James. This is a meal that James has been waiting for, and because he has enjoyed the first meal so much, he has been looking forward to having a home-cooked meal with Claudette again. James is sure he will not be disappointment; he knows that Claudette is a superb cook. Claudette has finished cooking, and James has finished setting the table for them to eat. They are now sitting and beginning to eat their dinner. After the meal, James and Claudette are engaged in conversation. James tells Claudette, laughing, "I got to stop coming to your house for dinner. I enjoy it too much. If I keep eating your cooking, I am going to become known as the fat man."

Claudette reaches over, squeezes James hand, and in between laughing, says, "There will be more to hug."

The two of them get a laugh out of the line of conversation as they begin to talk about their lives and their children's lives. James is already aware that Claudette is a widow for a little over two years; he recently has found out that she has two sons, one daughter, and five grandchildren. The two of them have completed their dinner and are now having desert and coffee during this informative conversation. James and Claudette are having so much fun talking with each other and really finding out much about each other that it eventually leads to James spending the night. The two of them soon find themselves in bed, making love for the first time; it is strange for Claudette because this is her first time making love with a man since the death of her husband. James is now the only man other than her late husband that she has ever made love with. It has also been awhile for James too now that he has changed his lifestyle from being a rather loose and not-so-choosey man for whom he is sleeping with. It is strange for both of them sleeping with someone. They enjoy the moment that eventually leads to a rather lengthy session of lovemaking. Neither of them wants it to end. Finally exhaustion ends lovemaking and sleep prevails.

The following morning, James is up early and finds out that Claudette is already up and cooking breakfast. The coffee is ready, and the remainder of the breakfast is just waiting for James. Claudette is just waiting for James to join her at the breakfast table. James tells Claudette, "Everything looks good and I bet the taste is just as great. I had better wash up so we can enjoy." James departs to wash up, and once he returns, the two of them sit to have breakfast. They are having an enjoyable morning talking and revealing themselves to each other by discussing events in their life before becoming widows. They soon complete breakfast. James is now realizing that he must head for home to prepare himself for work. Even though he does not want to leave Claudette, he knows that his leaving will be good. He knows that it will increase his thirst and desires to want to return just as soon as he can. As James is leaving, Claudette tells him that she enjoyed last night and hopes his night was just as enjoyable. James hugs Claudette and tells her in return how much he enjoyed not only last night but also life with Claudette as it is evolving, and just how strong his wishes are that this is the beginning of something wonderful and that all will continue. James kisses Claudette passionately as he departs for home, thinking just how nice it would be if he didn't ever have to leave Claudette.

James is now at work, thinking that just maybe he has finally found someone that will fill the missing peaces that his life has been missing. *Claudette makes me feel complete again.* James is much more pleasant to be with today and the office staff recognizes it. James just has to call Claudette so he dials her phone number.

Claudette answers the phone, "Hello!"

"I just could not wait any longer. May I ask are you doing?"

"Well I have been on the phone talking to my daughter most of the morning."

"Why don't you join me for lunch. Come by my office and we can have lunch."

"Where is your office? Oh, I think I have one of your cards with the address on it."

"If the address is not on it, let me know. You can just park in the building parking. We own the building, not the parking rights. We lease them but we can validate for you."

Claudette jokingly quips, "So you will pay for me to park, and I hope you will also take care of my lunch tab."

James jokingly replies, "I am the last of the big spenders."

"So I see, what is the suite number to your office?"

"My office is on the top floor. You can just come up to the top floor. My office is up there, and someone will direct you to me."

"What time should I arrive?2

"I would say that by noon, I will be ready."

"I see you at noon."

"I will be waiting!"

———∞———

After arriving and parking, Claudette takes the elevator up to James's office. She arrives on the penthouse level where

James's office located, and as she exits the elevator, she informs receptionist that she is there to see a Mr. James Lackey. The receptionist tells her to wait just a minute, and she calls James's executive assistant Mary Winfield to notify her that someone is there to see Mr. Lackey. Mary tells receptionist that she will be right there. Claudette sits and begins to observe the swanky layout. She is impressed.

Soon Mary arrives and says, "Mrs. Claudette Maddox?"

Claudette says, "Yes, that is me." Then they head James's office. They pass Joe Mills on the way. Mary introduces Claudette to Joe and tells her that Joe is James's son-in-law. Claudette shakes his hand.

The two of them proceed to James's office where they find James on the phone.

Mary says, "He is always on the phone."

"That is all right!" James realizes that Claudette has arrived and rushes to get off the phone. Mary tells James that Claudette met his son-in-law Joe on her way to see him.

James says, "Good! Are you ready for lunch?"

"Ready as I will ever be."

James tells Mary, "I will be out to lunch. Oh, by the way, Mary, this Claudette Maddox. Claudette, this is Mary Winfield, the woman that probably knows more about me than I know about myself." Claudette and Mary greet each other. James tells Mary that he will be having lunch at the restaurant that Mary has previously made reservations. "You know where to find me and call if you need me."

James and Claudette depart for lunch.

—⁂—

James and Claudette are having lunch, just talking about her first visit to James's office while they look at the menu.

Claudette says, "I hate to ask the old familiar question, but what is good here?"

"What do you like? The food here is mostly American. I eat here a lot."

"Well is there anything that you don't order?"

"I don't order the liver." He says with a smile on his face.

Claudette jokingly retorts, "Well, I guess I want to order the liver."

"Any dish you see on the menu that you think you might like is prepared well. I do not think you will go wrong ordering here."

"I think I will order fish!"

"An excellent choice. I think I will have the same thing. It is one of the house special today anyway."

James and Claudette finish ordering lunch and become engaged in chitchat about being prepared to retire when the time comes. James and Claudette both feel that neither of them is ready for retirement even though Claudette has not worked a steady job for any employer since her husband passed away. Prior to her late husband's death, Claudette has worked at the family accountant firm as a fulltime accountant partner with her husband. Finally James and Claudette finish their lunch and depart from the restaurant. James escorts Claudette to her car, and Claudette asks James if he would mind escorting her to an exhibit tonight where some young kids are displaying their artwork.

James says, "Tell me more about it."

Claudette shares, "These are kids that are living with single parents, poor surroundings, sometimes living in shelters. You know, needy kids that would be impressed seeing a successful person such as you."

"You talked me into it. Perhaps by attending, I can find out more about them. What time should I see you?"

Claudette writes down the address and says, "I will be already there. If you could meet me there around 6:00 p.m."

James realizes that he might have spoken too soon. "I think I had better check my calendar before I commit. I will have to call you to let you know. If I had known earlier, I would have scheduled it."

"I know this is late. If you can make it, fine, but if your schedule won't permit, I will understand."

"I am going to try to make it. I will call you."

She thanks James for lunch and says, "I enjoyed lunch." She then gives James a kiss on the cheek as she departs.

James returns to his office and checks his schedule to find out that he has scheduled a dinner with an old friend from college and high school days. James places a call to his old friend to reschedule dinner. James finds out that his friend is trying to contact him also to cancel dinner. This solves James problem. It works out perfectly for James. James admits to his buddy that his reason for calling is to reschedule the dinner. The two of them chuckle and agree to reschedule dinner. The two of them agree on a new date and time for the dinner, and after a bit of humorous chitchat about routine daily life, the two of them finally hang up the phone. James now realizes that he can now place the call to Claudette that he wanted to place all along and that is to let her know to let her that he will be able to make the art show.

Claudette is very happy to get the good news from James and thanks James. Claudette tells him that she will see him around 6:00 p.m. and that it is a dinner with sponsors and donors. "Don't worry about paying for anything. It is already paid for."

"Maybe I just might want to make a donation. That is if it is a good cause, and with your participation, I am sure the cause is good."

"It is one of my many projects that keep me busy."

"That is good. I need to be more active myself. I need to find some causes that I could feel good about."

"Well after my late husband passed, I had to find something to keep me busy that was away from the business that we had spent a lifetime building."

"That is very comforting to know and probably could have solved many of my problems."

"It was good for me. You know, I had better get off this phone and get ready."

"You are so right. I will see you around 6:00 p.m." Claudette agrees with James as she proceeds to give James all the relevant information about the event.

James once again tells Claudette, "I will see you at six," and then hangs up the phone.

The following morning, James finds himself waking up once again at the home of Claudette. Claudette is up and preparing breakfast for the two of them. James rushes to get out of bed because he knows that he will have to rush home again to get dressed for work, but he is not leaving before he enjoys the breakfast that Claudette has prepared. James and Claudette sit for breakfast and some conversation. James calls his office before they start eating and leaves a message for Mary that he might be running a little late but to call if she needs him.

"I know I have to be in court, but don't worry, I will be there." James concludes his call and returns to his conversation with Claudette as the two of them begin to eat their breakfast. James and Claudette soon finish breakfast.

Claudette, smiling, says, "I bet you could get use to waking up in the arms of an eloquent fine preserved older woman that have breakfast ready for you in the morning."

"Yep, you are spoiling me, and I am enjoying every minute of it. As a matter of fact, I am getting use to all of this pampering." He embraces Claudette and looking into Claudette's eyes says, "I must have you over to my house some time so I can prepare you a meal and pamper you."

"If that is a promise, I am going to take you up on it."

"Yes, that is a promise." He then gently says as he is embracing Claudette, "I wish I could stay longer, but I really must go."

Claudette sings, "Until the sun goes down and the lights are shining bright, we will meet again."

James, smiling, embraces Claudette again and places a kiss. "No matter how much I hate to say it, duty calls and I got to go." James departs as Claudette walks him to the door to watch him leave. She waves good-bye. James waves back at Claudette and throws her a kiss as he prepares his drive home to begin his day.

James arrives home, and there waiting for him is his youngest daughter Debbie, She immediately starts speaking in an angry tone of voice. "Dad, where have you been? We have all been worried about you. I have been calling you at home and on your cell phone with no answer."

James quickly responds, "Daddy is all right. I was out. I don't have much time for conversation. I have a court appearance in less than two hours."

"Daddy, you know we care about you, and you are not a young man!"

"Could we finish this conversation after we both fulfilled our daily obligations? I will be home early tonight. If you could hold the chitchat until I have time to talk."

Debbie responds, "Daddy, you know tomorrow is a school day. I won't have time to talk when you get home. The kids have homework and in bed by nine."

James says, "I will just have to make time. Call me. We will work something out." James is now getting ready for work. Debbie continues to try to get answers from James as he is trying to shower, shave, and get dressed. Finally Debbie realizes that she will not get answers to any of her questions and tell her daddy that she is not satisfied and will be back. Debbie is running late for work herself and has to leave. In route for work, Debbie places a call to her sister Pam to let her know that she has spoken to their father and that she is at his house when he arrived from some all-night affair, perhaps with one of those floozies. Pam asks Debbie if their dad has explained anything at all about the reason for his absence and not being around much lately. Pam tells Debbie that Joe had met and seen a woman by the name Claudette Maddox with their father at the office, and according to Joe, they were getting along pretty good. Debbie is now beginning to think that it is another woman and wants to know what she is like.

Pam says, "Joe tells me that she is a very attractive, eloquent older woman around Daddy's age."

Debbie replies, "Well at least he is picking somebody closer to his age."

"Maybe a relationship with a woman his age might be good for Daddy."

"Daddy does not need anyone. He has a family, and Mama is not cold in her grave yet."

"I have to go now. I am rushing to work, and I don't want to be late. I will call you later this afternoon."

"Bye, little sis, enjoy."

—⚌—

James makes his court appointment on time to appear before the judge in a civil case where his firm is representing a large corporation. This court appearance does not last very long. Once the court appearance is complete, James returns to his office for more preparation on the case. James arrives at his office to find out that there is a young man waiting for him by the name of Brad Maddox. James's assistant Mary Winfield informs James that this young man is waiting to see him. She tells James that he refuses to tell her his reason for wanting to see him and she can get rid of the young man if James does not want to see him, but James recognizes the name Maddox and wants to meet this young man. James tells Mary to show this young man into his office. The young man comes into James's office and politely introduces himself by saying, "Mr. Lackey, my name is Brad Maddox, and I understand you are a friend of my mother, Mrs. Claudette Maddox."

James's response is, "Your mom is a very nice and bright woman that I consider myself a very good friend with and enjoy keeping company with."

"I hope your intentions are to just see her at church and nothing else."

James says, "I am fond of Mrs. Maddox. She is a wonderful woman that I have a lot of respect for. My hopes are that you won't have a problem with that."

"Mr. Lackey, my mom is getting on in years. We lost my father a bit over two years ago, and she is just lonely."

"You might not know it, young man, but neither one of us is getting any younger. The time that the two of us spend together is like therapy for both of us. We both have a bit of living left in our lives."

Brad is not happy with what James is telling him. Brad says, "I don not think my mother should be doing any dating!"

"No one saying anything about dating. We are both lonely adults just looking for a little companionship. We just so happen to enjoy each other's company at church and even after we get out of church. I hope you can understand that."

Brad does not want his mom dating because he feels that his mom's loyalty should continue to be with his deceased father. Brad is showing anger, and it shows as he states to James, "I don't think you are listening to what I am trying to say. My mother does not need male companionship!"

"I do not want to sound disrespectful, but your mom is very decent and respectful woman that can decide for herself who she wants to have as a friend, and you should be happy that your mother is getting on with her life. You know, when she lost your dad, it was a very traumatic time in her life. She was lonely and continue to feels that she is all alone."

"She has a family. She is not alone."

"I lost my wife a little over two years ago, and believe me, we both understand the heartache that goes along with the loss of one half of your life. There are a lot of lonely days and nights that she is faced with."

Brad is not receptive to anything that James is saying and angrily says, "I must be going, and I hope you heard what I am saying." He storms out of James's office.

—⚭—

Immediately after Brad's departure, James places a call to Claudette and informs her of the visit that is just concluded by Brad. Claudette tells James, "Brad does not want me to have any friends, but don't worry, his bark is loud but his actions are zero."

James tells Claudette that he also have similar problems with his daughters. "As previously stated, I have two daughters. They are both married with two children each. Are there any other roadblocks in your life?"

Claudette's response is, "Yes, I have previously stated I have two more, a daughter and another son. My daughter is married with two children, and my other son is also married with three children. Brad is not married. He spends most of his time watching me. He does have a girlfriend who is very nice, and I am hoping he will announce his intentions with her." James suggests to Claudette that maybe the two of them should start thinking about meeting each other's family. They agree that it is a good idea. James tells Claudette that maybe she remembers meeting his son-in-law, also attorney by the name of Joe Mills who works at the firm. Claudette does remember him. She remember him. She remembers that James's executive assistant Mary introduced the two of them on her first visit to James's office.

James says, "He has noticed your visits to the office and has informed my daughters."

Claudette replies, "Well I am looking forward to meeting the rest of the family."

James jokingly quips, "When I meet the rest of your family, I hope my reception is much better than the one I received from Brad."

Claudette jokingly retorts, "Well, I think you will be pleasantly surprised with the rest of my family." Mary enters James's office and informs him that his daughter Debbie is on the phone.

James shares, "Speak of the devil, my youngest energetic one is on the phone now. I will call you later."

James answers the phone, "Hello, baby doll."

Debbie answers, "Hello Daddy, I have changed my mind. I can now meet you at home after work. What time do you plan to arrive home."

James says, "I have a bit more work, but I should be home no later than 6:00 p.m."

"I will meet you at six, don't be late."

"I will be there."

—⚏—

James arrives home with some carry-out food for his dinner. Debbie was waiting for him at his front door. James says, "Hello, baby doll, been waiting long?"

"No, I just arrived about two or three minutes ago."

James opens the door. "Come on in." The two of them entered the house. "Are you alone?"

"Yes, Daddy, I am alone. Do you see anybody with me?"

James pretends not to hear Debbie's answer, but instead, James says, I have dinner. I have plenty enough for both of us with leftovers."

"I accept. I will accept your offer. I am hungry." Debbie takes the food to the kitchen where she begins to inquire about where James has been spending his time lately and does he have something to tell the family.

"I would prefer to talk about it when Pam is present. I will then tell you whatever it is you want to know."

"Daddy, you must tell me something because Pam and I have been worried. Joe has been telling Pam that he has observed you and a woman leaving the office together on more than one occasion."

James tells Debbie that he would really like to talk about it when both she and Pam are present. Once again, he suggests that they all get together on the weekend. Debbie is not happy with this suggestion. Finally she agrees to do so but tells her dad that she would place a call to Pam and find out what her schedule is for the weekend. Debbie finishes preparing the food for them. The two of them sit at the kitchen table and begin eating the food. Debbie does not give up. She continues to talk about her concerns for her dad and his remaining loyalty to her mother. Debbie is trying to convince her Dad that what he is doing is hurting her and how much it must be hurting her mom. Debbie is telling her dad that he should try going to church sometimes.

James says, "If you had been in church every Sunday, you probably would have noticed I was there, and if you are there this Sunday, you will see me."

"You know I do not attend the same church as you." Some time later, Debbie and her Father finish eating. Debbie still is not happy. She says, "I have to go. I am going home." Debbie hugs her dad as she says bye.

"Say hello to Frank and the girls for me. Give the girls a great big hug for me and tell them that Grandpa loves them."

Debbie sarcastically quips, "They probably won't recognize you. After all, it has been a long time."

James ignores the comment. "Tell both of them that I will see them this weekend if their mom is not still angry with their grandpa."

"Bye, Daddy." She heads for her car, starts it up, and leaves in a hurry.

—◆—

It was Saturday morning, and James was at home sitting at his kitchen table with Claudette eating breakfast and drinking a cup of coffee when the doorbell rings. James arrives at the door to open it. To his surprise, Debbie was there unannounced. James says to Debbie, "Come into the house, baby doll. You will get your wish today." He and Debbie proceed to the kitchen where Claudette is sitting at the kitchen table, drinking a cup of coffee.

Debbie immediately walks over to Claudette, sticks her hand out, and introduces herself. "I am Debra Lackey-Samuels, the daughter of James and Margie Lackey."

CLaudette responds with, "I have heard all about you, and my name is Claudette Maddox, my friends call me Claudie."

Debbie immediately walks to another room where most of the family pictures are displayed and picks up a picture of her mom and dad together. She returns to kitchen and confronts Claudette by saying, "This is my mom and dad and this is their house. I just want to know what are you doing here without permission?"

James interrupts Debbie, but Claudette tells James to let her answer. Claudette says, "I am here because I was invited by your dad."

James raises his hand and states to Debbie, "Claudette does not have to explain her presence. She is here because

I invited her, and it does not require any explanation to my daughter."

Debbie says, "Fine, I am leaving, but it is not over with because I will stand by and allow another woman to just move into my mother's house and her body is not cold in the ground yet."

James says, "Debbie, I loved your mother very much and will always love her, but she passed away over two years ago. I believe I am not doing anything that she would not approve of. Claudette and I are both widowed, and we are both lonely for companionship. We enjoy being with each other and nothing that we are doing is harming anyone. You are my daughter and I love you very much. Just let me enjoy the life I have."

Debbie is not happy with the explanation, and it is evident as she heads toward the door and says, "Bye, Daddy."

James turns to Claudette and says, "She really is a good daughter."

Claudette responds with a smile and says, "I guess it will not be as easy as we would like. I guess love is not always easy." James was surprised to hear Claudette mention the word *love* between the two of them, but maybe she meant the love between a father and his daughter.

Debbie backs her car from the driveway and heads for home. She has decided to call her sister Pam. She begins by saying, "Pam, I just met the b——h."

Pam responds, "What b——h?"

"You know, the one that Joe has seen prancing around Daddy's office. She thinks she is going to just move into Mom's bed and we are going to stand back and do nothing."

"Debbie, you know Daddy is not going to take your butting into his business lightly. Why don't you just relax. Daddy is a big boy, and you should refrain from referring to Daddy's friend as a b——h because you do not know her well enough to have any kind of unconstructive opinion."

"Well I don't want to know her. The only thing is, I am not going to stand by and let no other woman move in and take the place of my mother. Maybe we should all get together as a family and have Daddy invite her to be present. Maybe then, only then, we will be able to let her know that her relationship with our daddy is not going to be easy."

Pam agrees that the entire family should get together with their daddy and his new woman friend but disagrees with Debbie and her effort to put an end to their daddy having a woman friend. Pam is of the opinion that a little companionship for her dad just might be good for him. Joe seems to be impressed with her daddy's choice of a woman friend this time. Pam realizes that her dad has made himself a little less available lately. Pam suggests to Debbie that she will call their dad and see if she can coordinate the family's schedule for a family get-together at her and Joe's home. Pam suggests her home because that way, she will have control over everything that takes place, and suggests maybe next weekend.

Debbie's response is, "I will make myself and my family fit the schedule anytime next weekend. You know Frank's schedule is as always is—either playing basketball or golf every weekend and if he is not playing basketball or golf, he is watching a game or golf with his boys down at that bar drinking beer."

Pam says, "Fine, I will get back with you either later today or tomorrow morning at church, just stay loose."

—◊—

A short time later, James receives a call from Pam. "Daddy, do you have a moment for your older daughter?"

James says, "Yes, baby girl, Daddy can always make time for either one of his favorite girls."

Pam says, "I will be over in about maybe twenty to twenty five minutes."

James says, "Okay." They say bye, and then he nods toward Claudette. James smiles at Claudette and says, "We had plans to meet each other's family. Well you met one today, and now you are going to meet the number 2 daughter."

Claudette looks at James and smiles and says, "Good, I am looking forward to it. I just hope this meeting will be much more receptive than the last one was."

James says, "You and I both hope this is not strike 3." The two of them laughs.

About twenty minutes later, James heard Pam's car pulling into the driveway and says to Claudette, "We are about to find out." The doorbell rings and James answers the door.

Pam gives her dad a hug and says, "Daddy, I have not had much Daddy time lately."

James says, "I guess that is a problem I will have to correct. How is my little Regina and Joe Jr.?"

Pam replies, "They are fine, just miss Grandpa." The two of them proceed to the den or sitting room where Claudette is sitting and now listening to music.

Claudette stands and starts to walk toward Pam with her hand out for a handshake but Pam says, with both arms out for a hug, "After all I have been hearing about you, I want a hug. My name is Pamela Lackey-Mills, the oldest daughter of James Earl Lackey."

Claudette and Pam meet with embrace and express to each other how happy they are to meet each other. Pam says, "I don't want to intrude on you guys. I just came by to check you guys' schedules for next weekend, and I wanted to do it in person, not on the telephone. I would like to invite you over to the house for one of Joe's grilled steaks so Claudette can meet the rest of our rude and mean family, at which time, maybe I can convince that other daughter to show up with her family. We can have a total Lackey family get-together inclusive of Mrs. Claudette Maddox." James looks at Claudette and they both nod, suggesting that they think it is a good idea.

Pam gives Claudette and James a hug and says, "I have to be leaving. My husband and those two that refer to me as *Mom* will be looking for me." Pam exits the house and leaves for home.

James and Claudette look at each other smiling. James says, "At least Pam has embraced our relationship." *Maybe this family gathering inclusive of Claudette that Pam is suggesting just might not be so bad after all.*

Monday morning, James sit in his office working as usual, taking phone calls and mingling with other office employees when his executive assistant Mary Winfield walks into his office to inform him that he is needed in a staff meeting. James responds with, "Tell them that I will be there shortly just as soon as I conclude this note to myself." The phone rings and Mary answers it in James's office and informs James that he has a phone call. James's response was, "Who is it?"

Mary asks, "Who may I say is calling?" Mary cupping the phone hands it to James and says, "It is that Brad fellow. You know, the one that came by to see you the other day. If you want me to get rid of him, I can."

James reaches his hand out and says, "I will take it." James places the phone to his ear and says, "James Lackey here, may I help you? No, I am about to go into a meeting, but if you want to meet with me, call back in about two hours. Better still, maybe we can have lunch, if that is okay with you. Just speak with Mary and she will arrange a lunch for say around twelve thirty. That's not good? You will be working? I was told that you and your lady friend are entertainers of some sort."

Brad answers, "That is not what I want to talk about, and you know it. You just want to duck the subject."

"Well what about a happy hour drink and maybe a bite to eat. Just let Mary know a good time for you."

"Okay, I will have to go now. They are waiting for me. Speak with my assistant, and she can arrange everything, bye." James passes the phone call to Mary as he departs for the meeting but first instructs her to make the reservation and place a call to Claudette to find out if she is available for a happy hour drink and maybe a bite to eat with Brad and him but not to tell Brad about Claudette. Mary tells James that she will take care of it, and not to worry, she will also take care of this Brad fellow.

James rushes off to his meeting. Some time later, at the conclusion of the meeting, James returns to his office and finds a note form Mary informing him that Brad had agreed to meet him around 5:30 p.m., and Claudette had also agreed to meet James at a favorite bar of Brad's that Claudette is familiar with and also a place that Brad and his woman friend Diana appear occasionally with their musical group in the bar as entertainers. This bar is located in a large well-known hotel that also serves food in its restaurant. The hotel is a part of a well-known chain. James is familiar with the hotel but has never been in the bar. James returns to his normal day of office work until he completes his day at the office. James proceeds to Claudette's house to pick her up. After picking Claudette up, the two of them leave her house and travel to the hotel to meet Brad at the bar. After arriving at the bar, James and Claudette decide to take a very comfortable seat on a large couch with a table available for their drinks and bar food to hold them in case Brad is late arriving. Shortly thereafter, a server arrives to take their order. James and Claudette place a drink order and request a menu as they sit there waiting for Brad. James and Claudette engage themselves in friendly conversation about what they think of Brad's response will be when he arrives and sees the two of them together. Brad is late, but they are patient as they wait. Finally after a couple of hours and still no Brad, James says to Claudette, "Maybe we have been stood up."

Claudette responds, "This is not like Brad. I know he is a bit of a hothead, but he is always dependable."

James says, "Well, he did not know you would be here and maybe it is his way of punishing me for being a love interest of his mom."

Claudette replies, "No, I do not think he would do that. This is not like my Brad. I believe something is wrong. I just cannot understand his reason for not calling you to explain. As a matter of fact, he has not called his mother today, and normally he calls me every day." The two of them continue to wait, limiting themselves to the bar food for dinner. It is now getting late, but at least the music in the background is pleasant. Finally, James pays the check and decides that it is

52

time to get out of the bar and takes Claudette home. James and Claudette arrive at Claudette's house. The two of them rush into the house. Claudette begins calling Brad, but there still no answer. She decides to call Diana, Brad's lady friend, and she has a bit of a time finding Diana's phone number, so she has decided to place a call to her daughter Peggy to see if she has decided to place a call to her daughter Peggy to see if she has Diana's phone number. Peggy does have a number of Diana. Claudette writes the number down and calls Diana to ask if she knows where brad is. Diana tells Claudette that she is also looking for Brad.

"He told me that he would call me to let me know the time he would be coming over. He was supposed to have a drink with someone first." Claudette explains to Diana that Brad was to meet with a friend of hers for a drink but he never did show up.

Claudette tells Diana that if she ever did get in touch with Brad to be sure to tell him to call his mama. Diana agrees to do so and says, "Yes, I will have him call you just as soon as I speak with him."

Diana and Claudette tell each other bye. It is now getting late. James tells Claudette that he will stay with her until she locates or contacts Brad. James could sense that Claudette is worried about Brad and is not going to rest until she finds out whether or not Brad is okay. Claudette continues to worries about Brad and soon finds herself getting sleepy but not wanting to fall asleep without hearing form Brad. She and James finally fall asleep on the couch, leaning on each other.

—⚉—

Early morning around 4:00 a.m., Claudette is unable to sleep when she hears the doorbell ring. Claudette jumps from the couch and runs to the door, hoping that it is Brad, with James following close behind her, but instead of Brad, it is a policeman, identifying himself as such. After finding out who she is being greeted by the policeman asks Claudette if he could come in and Claudette says, "Yes, you may."

The police officer tells Claudette that there has been a very bad accident and maybe her son is involved. The policeman asks Claudette if a Bradley Maddox is related to her and Claudette says, "Yes, that is my son. What is wrong and where is he?"

The officer tells Claudette that he has been taken to the hospital emergency. The officer states that they have been trying to locate his immediate family. Claudette is becoming emotional and asks the officer, "Is he all right?"

The officer says to her, "Do you have someone to drive you to the hospital?"

James steps forward and says, "I will drive Claudette." The officer apologizes for having to deliver the bad news, as he leaves. Claudette grabs her purse and puts her shoes on. James also rushes to put his shoes and jacket on. The two of them leave immediately for the hospital. They arrive at the hospital's emergency and rush inside to find out about Brad. The reception nurse tells them that she would make arrangements for them to speak with the doctor because Brad is still in recovery after some kind of surgery. As the time passes, Claudette is pacing back and forth in the waiting room and approximately forty-five minutes passed before a Dr. Stafford comes out to announce Claudette's name. Claudette rushes over to the doctor and introduces herself to the doctor. Dr. Stafford proceeds to inform Claudette that Brad is in extremely critical condition and that she see him but he will not be able to speak with her and will not know that she is present. Claudette is given directions by the doctor where Brad's room is located and where she can visit Brad.

Once James and Claudette reach Brad's room, she becomes very emotional after observing Brad's condition and is being restrained in the waiting room, where Claudette's son Pearce Maddox II and his wife Brenda and Claudette's daughter Peggy Olsen have arrived and want to know how Brad is doing. Claudette's response is, "I am loosing my baby." Pearce rushes over to his mother to console her and Peggy also proceeds to be by her mother's side. Pearce, Peggy, and Brenda are told that they will be granted a visit with Brad. After their visit to see Brad, they all come away very distraught. A short time later, Diana Woods, Brad's girlfriend, and Jim Olsen, husband of Peggy, arrive and Diana wants to know how Brad is doing and wants to visit with him. Diana goes to Brad's room and does not want to leave. She is saying that she is not going home after observing Brad's condition. The hour is getting later. The morning has arrived and is getting late.

The nurse on duty tells the family that they should all go home and get some rest because Brad is in good hands. "We will call if Brad's condition changes."

Claudette is very emotional, saying, "I am not leaving. I want to be here with him."

Diana is equally as loud with her response of, "I am not leaving either." After a period of time, most of the family is convinced that maybe there is nothing they can accomplish by staying at the hospital and head for home. Finally Claudette and Diana arrive at the same conclusion—that it is probably best that they also go home and get some rest.

It is already morning time and almost time for James to be getting into his office. James instead decides to take the day off. He calls Mary and tells her what has happened and cancel his appointments for the day and that he will be with Claudette, so if the office needs him, just give him a call. After spending the remainder of the morning at the home of Claudette, he decides to go home and freshen up with a shower, shave, and fresh clothes. James rushes to his house and quickly gets dressed for his return to be with Claudette. James rushes back to Claudette's home, but when he arrives, Claudette has already left home. James assumes that she has left for the hospital, so he leaves for the hospital, and when he arrives, he finds out that he was right in his assumption. James makes an attempt to console Claudette, but she is not receptive to his presence and asks James if she could speak with him outside of Brad's room. The two of them go into the waiting room and have a seat. Claudette tells James that maybe her relationship with him contributed to Brad's accident. James's response was, "What do you mean?"

Claudette says, "Well you know how much he disapproved of our being together. Maybe we should put the brakes on our relationship. I am not going to be very much fun as long as Brad is in the condition that he is in, so please forgive me. You know, I was beginning to fall head over heels in love with you even at this advanced age."

James embraces Claudette and expresses his feelings for her and says, "I just wanted to be there for you during this time of need. You know the feeling is mutual on this love thing. I was beginning to feel that my life was restored to what they call it, you know, 'Happy days are here again,' but if you think you need a little time, I will be here if you need me. Just keep me informed on Brad's condition."

Claudette never did answers Jame's request too keep him informed on Brad's condition. James decides that it is not a good time to become involved in any further discussion with Claudette, because she is not thinking soundly. James immediately leaves the hospital and heads for home.

CHAPTER

3

As time passes, James neither sees Claudette nor hears from her even though he has made many attempts to contact her. Claudette even stops attending church service. Her church attendance and activities have always been a main part of her life. It is difficult to understand this Claudette. Maybe she is having health problems. It is hard to believe that Claudette has just quit on everything that has always been such a big part of her life. Occasionally, James will take a drive by her home, thinking that maybe he might catch a glimpse of Claudette either entering or leaving her home. James also sometimes drives out of his way to shop for food in the neighborhood supermarkets that Claudette usually shops. James not thinking of giving up on Claudette because he still believes that Claudette does not just cut short a relationship that she is just beginning to feel comfortable with. James finally reluctantly decides that if Claudette ever wants to contact or see him, she knows his number, and he will be ready to take her call.

—〰—

James is having lunch with some of his office staff, celebrating a staff birthday when he notices a familiar face. It is the face of a young woman attorney by the name of Jennifer Holt located at a table near where his party is seated. James speaks to Jennifer, which leads the beginning of a conversation about an old case where the two of them first met representing opposing clients. The conversation continues for the duration of their meals. James eventually finds himself continuing the conversation with her after his office staff has departed. Jennifer is also alone by now, because everyone with her has also excused themselves which leads to James joining Jennifer at her table. Their conversation must have been boring to everyone else as it consisted mostly of pass experiences in their chosen professions. They finally conclude their conversation at the valet while picking up their cars. They exchange business cards with each other. James says as the valet is delivering his car, £We won't have to look up old files to know how to contact each other now that we have exchanged business cards." Jennifer agrees with James as the valet is also delivering her car. The two of them departs for their offices and their work for the remainder of their day.

Claudette is sitting with Brad at the hospital, wondering if James has moved on with his life now that she has refused to communicate with him. Brad's condition has improved enough that the doctors are saying that he might be going home soon. Brad wakes up from a sleep and recognizes his mom sitting next to his bed. Brad says, "Hello, Mama, how long have you been here?"

Claudette responds, "Long enough to watch you sleep peacefully."

"I fell asleep this morning because I could not sleep during the night."

"Why couldn't you sleep?"

Brad smiles, "I was awake watching television."

"You might be going home soon. That is if your condition continues to improve."

"The doctor tells me that I am doing well. I still feel stiff, but most of broken bones are healing good."

A nurse enters room to check brad's vitals and to give Brad some medication. At the same time, Diana enters Brad's room and speaks with Claudette and Brad. The nurse finishes with Brad's vitals and is now administering his medications. She finishes and exits the room. Diana, leaning over to give Brad a kiss, asks, "How are you feeling today?"

"I am doing fine. I just might be going home soon."

Claudette says to Diana, "If he is this demanding here at the hospital, I can only imagine what he is going to be like at home."

"Both of you will be there with me and happy that I am home."

Claudette says, "We might be glad that you are home, but waiting on you is a no, no."

Diana says, "I have not had any breakfast. Mrs. Claudette, do you mind going with me to the cafeteria?"

Claudette responds, "I can get me something to drink."

Claudette and Diana tell Brad that they will return shortly.

"I will be here waiting."

—⁓—

Diana and Claudette enter the hospital cafeteria and proceed to the food line. Diana is purchasing food, and Claudette only purchases a cup of coffee. They finally proceed to find a table to consume their food and drink. Diana says, "Mrs. Claudette, I want to ask you something. Whatever happened to that nice looking man that I met the night of Brad's accident?"

Claudette responds, "Well I have not seen him lately. He is a busy man."

"I thought you guys had something going on, you know, seeing each other."

"Well we had been seeing a bit of each other, but since Brad's accident, Brad is more important."

"Didn't you care about him? He seemed like a nice man."

"He is very nice, a widow just like me. His wife passed shortly after my late husband Preston, and even though we attend the same church, we never did know each other. I did see Mr. Lackey—his name is James Lackey—and his late wife.We just never did develop any friendship with each other."

"How did you guys finally get together?"

"Well that is a story I will tell you about another day so we can have something to talk about next time."

"I am going to hold you to it." Their conversation continues.

It was late afternoon. Most of the office staff has left for the day, and just before James is about to conclude his day's work and heads for home, the phone rings. James answers the phone. The caller is the young female attorney, Jennifer Holt, on the line. She identifies herself by saying, "This is Attorney Jennifer Holt. You remember me?"

James says, "I certainly do. How did you know that I would be answering the office phone at these late hours?"

"I really did not think you would answer the phone. I was just taking a chance to see if you were still around."

"Now that you have me on the line, what can we do for you? Not very many of our staff is still around. Mostly everybody has left for the day."

"I was hoping that I would catch you or at least leave you a message. I would like to get together with you whenever you can find time to discuss a case that I am handling. I have been told that the subject matter just so happens to be one that you have had a lot of experience handling."

"Someone has confidence in me. I am not sure what the subject is. When is a good time for you?"

"I have been trying to get in touch with you for some time now. It seems that you are a busy man. I just want to pick your brains, say maybe over dinner."

"Having dinner with you would be a pleasure. Guys my age are going to wonder what a beautiful young woman is doing with me. I have been hearing many good things about you and your career. Everyone tells me that you have a bright future."

"I am not that young, and sometimes, my future seems to have reached its peak."

James tells Jennifer, "I am not doing anything after I leave here, and if you are not busy this evening, maybe the two of us can grab a bite to eat this evening."

"I will take you to dinner!"

"I accept. Is there any preparation that I need and where will we be eating?"

"Do you like Italian food?"

"I love good Italian food."

"Okay, I know the perfect place that I use to frequent with my dad that is very quiet. I can meet you there, say around seven?"

"Perfect, just give me the address." Jennifer reads the address to James. The address sounds familiar to James. He recognizes it the former favorite eatery of his and Margie. "I will have just enough time to wrap up what I am doing. I will see you at seven."

"See you then." She then hangs up the phone. James is now thinking that a visit to a favorite restaurant of his and Margie and having a dinner with another woman that is much younger than him will rekindle old thoughts of Margie that will not be pleasant. Maybe Margie would think this is a bad idea, and now what about his newfound interest in Claudette? Thinking to himself, *Well maybe Claudette has drawn a line through my name and forgotten who I am. Anyway, I need a night out, and maybe a dinner with another woman is just what I need. My daughters will find me easier to get along with. Why should I be worrying about having dinner with a fellow attorney? This is not a date. It is just a pretty face and body with a bright legal mind that is probably married with a husband and a couple of little ones at home.*

James arrives at the restaurant and is immediately recognized by the hostess; James also recognizes Jennifer is waiting for him at the bar, where he proceeds to greet her. Jennifer informs the hostess that she can seat the two of them now, which she does. They begin their conversation. At which time, Jennifer tells James that she has observed him at this restaurant in the pass. James tells Jennifer that it was a favorite eatery of his and his late wife, and on occasion, he continues to visit because he loves the food. The waiter comes over with menus and recognizes James and speaks to him.

Jennifer says, "Well I guess you are known here." The conversation is lively and friendly. Jennifer informs James that she has respected him and his work and knows all about James Earl Lackey for some time now. She knows just how respected James is in the legal profession and how much his law practice has grown over the years to one of the largest and most respected and prestigious law firms in the country. James begins to blush and says thank you but also telling Jennifer that she is also making a name for herself.

Jennifer says, "I am doing okay. My hard work has not been very good for my social life, and you know, all work and no play."

"I would think a beautiful young woman like you would be selecting any young man that she wants."

"I don't have the time for a social life, and whenever I do get a chance to go out with someone, they never call for a second date."

"I know many young men that would be only too happy to date a pretty, young, and intelligent attorney such as you."

"Date me once and find out that I am boring, never again."

The food server arrives to take their orders. The two of them place their orders with the server and continue their conversation until the food arrives at which time they start eating and enjoying their meals with continued conversation until they have both finished their meals. The server returns with the desert menu but neither of them orders desert. They both order coffee. Finally the two of them conclude the evening and not discussing Jennifer's reason for wanting to meet with James. The two of them say goodbye to each other after agreeing to another get-together to answer Jennifer's questions. James and Jennifer are expressing how much fun the evening has been and how informative the casual meeting has been. It seems that both of them needed a night out. James and Jennifer finally depart the restaurant. James drives home, and after a short while at home, he begins to prepare for bed. All of a sudden, he starts to think about Claudette. *Maybe I will give her a call, but she is probably in bed.* However, he decides to place a call to her anyway but finds out her phone number has been disconnected with no forwarding number. James believes now more than ever that Claudette has decided to move on with her life without him. He is awake for a while, unable to fall asleep, wondering what is next for him. James finally falls asleep.

—⁓—

About a week passes, James receives a call form Jennifer inviting him out for dinner. James agrees but tells Jennifer that he is paying this time. James soon finds himself meeting Jennifer fairly often and developing a social life, which means that they are now spending time together outside of their professional life. Jennifer's legal questions have been answered for some time now, and there is no further legal help that James is providing Jennifer. James and Jennifer soon find themselves waking up in bed together.

Jennifer says, "I hope last night was fun to you."

James responds, "I was wondering if you enjoyed yourself last night, especially before we fell asleep."

"Last night was wonderful, and I am feeling protected waking up wrapped up in these two strong arms." Jennifer is rubbing James's arms.

"I could just lie here all day."

"I could do likewise, but duty calls, I have a nine o'clock appointment."

"I must admit, duty calls for me too." He looks at Jennifer and gives her a little kiss on the lips. James and Jennifer are now seeing each other regularly, mostly as sexual partners, not lovers. They are spending their off-duty time with each other mostly in bed. They soon realize that there is no chance of romance developing in their relationship, just that the sex is good. They also realize that they can take advantage of this relationship for convenience purposes, like having a built-in date if ever the need arises. Also, the understanding that whenever either one of them is in need of or desires for sex, they can always call each other. Jennifer really is a pretty face with a good figure. James is a distinguished handsome older gentleman to Jennifer, but the two of them having nothing in common with each other but sex.

Now that the fling with Jennifer is understood with no romantic attachments. James begins meeting other women, and most of the time, they also are much younger than James. He is thinking that maybe he is just having a lot of fun with no attachment. Most of the women are satisfying his sexual needs, and whenever necessary, James has a pretty young woman on his arm to be seen out on a date with and not necessarily Jennifer because James is seeing less of Jennifer these days. Needless to say, Pam and Debbie are not happy with their father being seen with women even younger than the two of them and all of the conversation about him that goes along with it.

Debbie starts to tell Pam, "At least that Mrs. Claudette is his age."

Pam replies, "Maybe our daddy represents what I have always heard about older men, and these younger women are just looking for a sugar daddy."

"I don't like it!"

"I am just going to learn to live with it and let Daddy get it out of his system. I wonder what happened between him and Mrs. Claudette. She seemed like such a nice fit for Daddy."

"Daddy needs to grow up, and I am going to tell him so."

James is now starting to do a bit of pleasurable traveling, and at times, he takes one of his much younger women with him, which provides for many confrontations and disapprovals by his daughters. James is currently taking a trip on a luxury cruise ship with a young woman friend by the name of Karen Chambers, one of the beautiful young women that James has been dating lately. Karen is a young, beautiful, sexy woman that seems to do wonderful things for a bathing suit and is not ashamed to show her figure off. Karen is enjoying herself, by trying to enjoy as many events and sights the cruise had to offer, which is cause for James to be up late at night dancing, drinking, and having a lot of sex with Karen. He is meeting other couples, and on occasion, some of his new friends would mistake Karen for his daughter. This does not hurt James's feelings. He instead feels good about the fact that a man his age could pal around with this young beautiful woman. Karen is always happy, outgoing, and very likeable. She spends a lot of time sightseeing and shopping during the ship's dockings, and at night, it is partying with James until late at night and lot of sex early in the morning. James soon gets a little tired of this kind of life even though it is temporary and supposed to be fun. James continues to make an attempt to enjoy his trip along with Karen. Sometimes James just wanted to relax, go to bed early, and get up for breakfast just as he would if it is Margie with him instead of Karen. As time passes and the end of the cruise is arriving, James and Karen are packing to exit the ship and head for home. Karen is telling James how much fun the trip has been for her and that she enjoyed spending quality time with him and maybe this can lead to something good in the future. James is thinking that he knows his family is going to be upset with him for being away and not contacting any of them. If they are able to find out about Karen being in the picture, it will not make things any easier. James and Karen become engaged in some pleasant conversation. James lets Karen know how much he has enjoyed this trip, but deep down inside, James did not feel that the two of them have very much of a future together and is glad the cruise is over. James leaves the cruise ship without any plans to see Karen socially in the future. Karen leaves the cruise ship with high hopes of continuing and developing a romantic relationship.

Claudette is beginning to agonize over how she treated James and maybe it was not the wisest decision that she could have made. Her life is miserable. She is allowing Brad to control her decisions. After all, he is her son and she only wants to make him happy. On this day, her son, Pearce, is visiting with her, wondering why his mom has discontinued attending church service. Claudette is explaining to Pearce that her primary obligations are to Brad right now. "My plans are to resume all of my activities once Brad has fully recovered and back to himself. Right now, he needs me."

"Mom, you have a life too. If Brad needs someone around, call me, or Peggy, and I am sure Diana is available too."

Brad says, "Big Bro, just stay out of this. We are doing fine."

Pearce responds, "You are not that bad off. You are not totally helpless. Give mom a break. She gets tired too."

Claudette interrupts, "I do not want you boys arguing. Everything is fine. I am fine."

Pearce says, "Mom, I just want you to be comfortable now. If Daddy was here. He would not allow Brad to get away with all of these childish demands."

Brad retorts, "If Daddy were alive, I would not have ever been in that accident in the first place."

Pearce demands, "How would Daddy have prevented you from the accident?"

"Mama would nor have been out dating another man."

Claudette asserts, "Mr. Lackey had nothing to do with your accident."

"Mom, who is that Mr. Lackey?"

"He is an attorney and also a widow. You met and might not remember, but he and I were together the night of Brad's accident. He came to the hospital with me and was there with us throughout the night. HE also attends the same church that your daddy and I attended, and I continue to attend. We have enjoyed a few lunches and dinners together. He is very nice, and he is lonely the same as me."

Brad says, "You do not need any boyfriend. You are getting old."

Pearce says, "I think I remember Mr. Lackey. He seemed like a nice gentleman. Mom, if you need some companionship with a gentleman close to your age, there is nothing wrong with it. Daddy left us now for over two years and getting closer to three."

Brad shouts, "I say no!"

"Mr. Lackey and I have not seen each other since the morning after Brad's accident. I am sure he has found many things to occupy his time now. I have moved on just as I am sure he has."

"Whether Mr. Lackey has moved on or not, I don't want Brad placing all of these demands on you. I want you to resume your life as a happy, contented woman, and if you want to see Mr. Lackey again, you have my support."

"I am not in support of her seeing that Mr. Lackey. He doesn't need our mama. He probably has plenty women."

"I am happy, Pearce!"

"What is important to me is your happiness, and I do not believe this has made you happy."

"Thank you, Pearce, but I am okay."

James is home. After some time passes and he does not hear from his family, James decides that he should let his family know that he is home from his cruise, even though he did not tell them where he disappeared to. James finds out as expected that his family is upset with him for pulling such disappearing act. He has disappeared for seven days and has not call or let either of his daughters or anyone else in his family know where he was at, only telling them that he had to get away for some alone time. Debbie is her usual self, accusing her dad of spending time with some other floozies and ignoring his family. Pam much more levelheaded is just wondering if her daddy is safe in whatever he is doing or with whom. She does not want her dad's actions to be unsafe. James knows that what he is doing does not meet with the approval of his daughters. His real problem is living his life without Margie, the woman that he has always loved. James feels that he has already met the woman that perhaps could make him happy again and fulfill all of the needs that a man reaching his senior years in life would need, but now she has excluded him form her life and he cannot get in touch with her, James considers what he is doing is moving on with his life, and if he was able to find satisfaction and happiness once, maybe satisfaction and happiness are not that far down the road again.

James is now getting on with his life even though it is not exactly what he is happy with. James is now beginning to receive phone calls form his recent cruise date, Karen Campbell. James is still hoping that Karen is satisfied and can resume her life without him. The cruise is over, and he is not interested in continuing a relationship with her. James made many excuses for not being available to see her or answering her phone calls. James figures Karen would forget him. After all, she is a beautiful young woman and would have no problem getting a nice young man her age. Karen continues to call him anyway, and finally one day, she appears at James's office. She is told that James is not available. She proceeds to make a spectacle of herself, using profanity, making claims that James wants her when the two of them are on that cruise ship, and before she could get too far out of hand, James appears and rushes her into his office and closes the door.

James says to Karen, "Just settle down. What can I do for you?"

Karen has toned her voice down a bit and asks James, "Why can't you return just one of my f——king phone calls?

When we were shacked up on that cruise ship, you did not complain when I was f——king you every morning."

James is a little embarrassed and does not want anyone in his office to hear the profanity. He tells Karen, "You know there is a big difference in our ages. If you remember while we were on that cruise ship, people often mistook you as my daughter. How do you think I felt?"

"Your age is only a number to me!"

"My age is a great big number and yours is a small number."

"I realized that your age is a lot greater than mine, but it didn't matter. If you want to be with me anymore, all you have to do is tell me. I can get another man. I thought you were special. And, yes! I was impressed with you and thought that just maybe the two of us might have a chance at something special. Right now, I do not feel wanted, so as far as I am concerned, you can go f—— yourself. I am out of here."

James, afraid that Karen would not leave quietly, says to Karen, "Don't leave angry. I want you to know that I enjoyed being with you on that cruise. You presented me with some very memorable and enjoyable moments that I will never forget."

"You could have prevented all of this form happening, and I would not have had to come down here and embarrass you and me."

"I am sorry. I know it was wrong of me."

"So if you don't think we have a chance, I am as I just said outta here!" Karen heads for the door and tells James not to call her now because it won't do any good.

James says, "I am sorry you feel that way."

"I can let myself out." James is still startled and is wondering what kind of a mistake has he made.

—ᴡ—

James returns to work after his encounter with Karen, and while busy trying to catch up on what he had missed during his absence, James's son-in-law, Joe Mills, has come into James's office and says, "I am told that I just missed the big show. I am glad I was not around. I won't tell anybody! Do you have a minute?"

To which James says, "Come on in. Have a seat. Yes, it was just one of my many mistakes in life. This will teach me to be more careful about whom I make friends with."

"What happened and where did you meet her?"

"I am not sure. She just happened. What can I do for you?"

"Your daughters are very upset with you, and I am the chosen one to talk with you."

"I know I have not made myself available much lately but I plan to change. How is little Joe Jr. and Regina?"

"Nothing that a little time with Grandpa could not repair. Joe Jr. is still involved in sports and now Regina is playing basketball. They both would be happy if
Grandpa would come out to see them play."

"When do they have a game?"

"I will e-mail a copy of their schedules to you."

"That will be nice, and I promise that I will place their games on my priority schedule. So what are the messages that you have form my two watchdogs?"

"They are both worried about you. Pam is more worried for your safety. Debbie, I don't have to explain. She is wild right now. You can imagine what she is saying. I truly believe that if you start to spend a bit more time with the grandchildren, most of your problem would be solved, not necessarily true with Debbie, but it will be a start."

"Those two will want to take more control over my personal life. I love them dearly, but I have been trying to put their mom's death behind me. As you know, she was the only girlfriend I ever had and the only woman that I ever slept with all of our lives together. I loved her very much, and I still miss her."

"I do not think either of them doubts your love for mom. It is that they believe you have made up your mind to exclude your family form your life."

"I have been trying to develop some kind of social life for myself that probably as you can tell by this recent action taking place in my office is not going very well. I promise you that I will include my family in my life from now on. I just want you to let the two of them know that if I have a social life that the two of them do not have approval rights and they must understand."

"I will do that, and they will understand, at least Pam will, and I hope Debbie will also but you know how she feels about her mom and dad's life together." At this time, Joe tells James thanks, and he will let them know all about the conversation. "I had better get back to work. I will e-mail those schedules to you. I am involved in that Schumate case, you know." He then leaves James's office.

James is at his desk working and calls Mary into his office. He asks Mary to schedule a meeting for him. At the same time, he receives a call from his sister Mary Chambers, asking him if he could spend a little time with her and her family next month. James asks her what is the occasion, date, and time.

Mary says to James, "Well, you know, Jack and I will be celebrating our thirty-fifth wedding anniversary on the twenty-fourth of next month, and we have decided to have a small at-home family get-together, you know, have all the kids and grandchildren and of course you and your family."

"What about your big brother?"

"You know I am not forgetting them. They are invited, and the twenty-fourth is a Saturday around five. You are allowed to bring a friend." She chuckles. "You know, I keep hearing from Pam and Debbie that you are becoming quite a lady's man even at your advanced age."

"I will definitely put the date on my schedule. I don't think you should pay much attention to Pam and Debbie. I hate to sound as if I am trying to rush you, sis, but you know how it is with this hard working man. Someone is waiting my services." He slightly chuckles. "Man has to work, you know! I will see you on the twenty-fourth if not sooner." James hangs up the phone with his sister and begins thinking about Claudette, wondering if she has completely forgotten about him, the feelings that he has acquired for her in the short period of time that the two of them spent together. This as also evident in all of his daily actions and feelings. James knows and understands that he has to continue to face up to reality, and keep on living.

CHAPTER

4

Claudette and her daughter Peggy are in a supermarket shopping for grocery and talking when Peggy asks her mom why she has not been participating or attending church services lately. Peggy knows how important her mom's church services and activities have always been to her. Peggy asks her mom why the big change in her life and why all of a sudden church is not important. Claudette responds with, "My faith is and always be very important to me. You know I really don't have a good excuse for my lack of involvement. It is just that I have not been in much of a mood for anything since Brad's accident.

"Well, Mom, you and Dad have always been active in your church. I was of the opinion that church and faith are now more important than ever since we lost Dad."

Claudette realized that she and Peggy are blocking the aisle with people trying to shop and says, "We had better move, honey. We need to move out of these people's way." Peggy realizes that her mother does not want to continue answering all of her questions and suggests that the two of them proceed to the checkout and to pay.

—w—

Once the two of them reach the checkout, Claudette says to Peggy, "Well you know I miss your dad very much. We had been together since high school except for the time he spent serving his military tour of duty, and then he would write to me almost every day." Claudette is being a little hesitant in her delivery to Peggy but feels that she has to get it out anyway. "I met a man by the name of James Lackey, an attorney that also attends the same church as me. He lost his wife a few years ago. Now this a man that I had seen for years with his wife as members of the church congregation together many times, but I had never spoken to either of them until a few months ago. James and I sat next to each other one Sunday and started to talk not during services or whenever there was a break. After church services were over, we decided to have a bite to eat together. We soon found out that the two of us suffers from the same loneliness. We had both lost our spouse. If you remember, Mr. Lackey was at the hospital with me after Brad's accident. He attempted to be with me afterward, but I thought it best that I discontinue any possible relationship before one of us gets hurt, so I have not seen him since."

Peggy asks her mom, "Why don't we go over to the coffee shop and have a cup so we can talk?" The two of them proceed to check out and proceed to the coffee shop to have a cup of coffee. They are also having a snack. After talking for a while about why Claudette tells Peggy as politely as she can about Brad's feelings about her seeing another man, or her developing any kind of relationship with any man. Peggy tells her mom that she feels that a complete social life is exactly what she needs.

Half eating her snack and drinking her coffee, Claudette interrupts Peggy and says, "You know Brad is going to be worried about me. He was not expecting me to be away this long."

Peggy says, "Well he has his sweetie poo Diana with him. He won't miss you. I do want to know more about this attorney James Lackey."

"Well we had plans for a Claudette and James family introduction dinner. As I just explained, Brad was not happy with me seeing another man. I never got the chance to tell him about the family get-together, which was our plan the night Brad suffered his injury. Our plan was to meet with Brad together, even though we had not told him. Mind you, Brad had been outspoken in his objections to anything between James, I mean, Mr. Lackey, and I ever happening. The accident prevented that meeting from ever happening. James has two daughters, which I met and was received very well by his oldest daughter but the youngest was as stubborn and as much against Mr. Lackey and I being together socially as Brad."

Did Brad meet Mr. Lackey?"

"Yes, Brad has even been over to James's office to express his displeasure." Peggy asks her mom if her brother Pearce had met Mr. Lackey. "Pearce has not met Mr. Lackey formally, other than the two of them along with you being in the hospital after Brad's accident. You know, things were so chaotic that morning that no one remembers very much outside of the perceived condition of Brad. Pearce has been told about Mr. Lackey."

Peggy wants to know even more about Mr. James Lackey. She wants to know if her mom continues to have any interest in him and why he has not been around the family especially during these trying times and just maybe she and Pearce could also meet. Claudette's response is, "Well, you know, I do not want to upset Brad. He has been going through a lot lately."

"Well if it serves as any inspiration for you, I will talk with Brad and remind him that you have a life also. I want to meet Mr. James Lackey, maybe my future daddy." she says with a smile.

"He has probably forgotten all about me and has other interest other than your mother. Remember, I am not getting young. It is old that I am becoming."

"Mom, you are not old. You could even pass for my younger sister."

Claudette is blushing. "I guess we had better go before the two of us is chastised by your little brother. You know how he has been lately. He is probably sitting there getting angrier by the minute."

"Mom, you are taking care of Brad in your house. You are the mom and he is the son living with you under your rules, so relax, if need be, I will be with you. You know Brad doesn't give me no trouble."

"I will be all right, honey. It was good spending this time with you, and maybe we can do this more often, you know, get together, but I really do have to go."

"Okay, Mom, I will take my few groceries home and hug my husband and kids. I will be over soon to speak with Brad."

Claudette hugs Peggy and says, "Bye, baby!" Peggy says bye as the two of them departs.

—⁂—

Few days pass and Claudette is home having breakfast with Brad, who is visibly disabled from the accident. She is pretending to read the morning newspaper and also aid Brad in his attempt to eat his breakfast. Claudette mentions to

Brad that she is wondering if James is seeing someone else, Brad says, "Mom, I need you. That Mr. Lackey has plenty of friends and a lot to keep him busy. I understand his daughters are not happy with him being with you anyway. I wish you would forget him because I need you." Claudette just nods to Brad and goes back to reading her newspaper at which time her doorbell rings, and when Claudette opens the door, as expected, there was Brad's girlfriend Diana and Claudette's daughter Peggy. Diana has been there for Brad and feels that Brad is preventing his mother from being happy—all of his daily constant demands on her time. He does not even want his mom to attend church due to the possibility of her coming in contact with Mr. James Lackey. Brad does not want his mom to even attempt to see or call James to give him an explanation why she has not been willing to see him.

Peggy asks Brad, "How are you feeling today, little brother?

Brad's response is, "You know I can't do anything. I am just here, and if it wasn't for Mom, I don't know what I would do."

"Well you know that there are other ways for you to be provided for so Mom can have a life. The life she deserves."

Brad becomes agitated and says, "The only thing you want is for me to be shuffled off to the side, but Mom will never push me off to the side. You can go on about your business. I will be okay."

At which time, Diana interrupts and says, "Brad, you know I will never leave you, but your mom does need a life other than staying here with you 24-7. I wish you would lighten up."

Claudette says, "Brad and I are fine, and I do have a life. Do you girls want some breakfast? I have enough for both of you."

At which time, Diana says, "I will a cup of coffee and maybe a little of that fruit."

Peggy says, "I will a little coffee also, but I want the breakfast. Everything you guys are eating." Diana and Peggy join Brad and Claudette at the kitchen table for breakfast. Claudette places settings for Diana and Peggy to eat.

Peggy says, "Mom, sit down. We can get our own place settings!"

Claudette replies, "I am fine, dear. I have everything now, so sit and eat." They all begin to eat. As time passes, the conversation eventually leads to Peggy asking her mom if she has been attending church lately. She just wants to see how brad is going to react. Claudette's response is that she has been spending most of her time with Brad.

Claudette says, "You know someone has to be here with Brad at all times. You know he has to be taken to therapy and doctor's appointments, plus all the medications that he is taking for his pain. I have to prepare his meals."

Brad agrees, "Yes, Mom takes good care of me, and I don't know what I would do without her. She does not have time for church."

Diana says, "Brad, I am here for you. Your mom can go to church and if you need someone to be with you, I am here."

Brad says, "You got a job to perform every day and so does Peggy. Both of you have to go to work. You don't have time the time to be here with me."

Diana responds, "Brad, you know I do not work on Sundays when Mrs. Maddox attends church services."

Peggy says to Brad sarcastically, "Whatever Brad, you don't need as much help as you are demanding. There are some things you can do for yourself. Lots of people are in wheelchairs, and I do believe you can get out of that chair if you really want to. I spoke with your therapist, and he tells me that you are doing really good and can walk if you want to. He tells me that you walk every time you are working out with him."

Brad says, "My momma loves me and she sees my progress firsthand. Yes, I can walk little bit, but I need more time."

"Brad, you know I do not work on Sundays during church hours, and I could at least be with you long enough for Mrs. Claudette to attend church service."

"You are welcome to be here with Mama too."

Peggy seeming a little frustrated with her brother says, "Mom, thanks, I am leaving, and thanks for the breakfast." Peggy hugs her mom, Diana, and Brad, and says, I is out of here,"

Diana tell Peggy, "We are going to improve these conditions. I will be here for a while working on it. Sometimes I wonder why, but you know I love your brother." Peggy leaves Claudette, Brad, and Diana. Claudette and Diana are now putting the leftover food away, cleaning up after the breakfast, as they continue talking.

Saturday the twenty-fourth has finally arrived, and James is arriving at his sister and brother-in-law's house with a lady friend by the name of Melody Farrell who is much younger and as usual attractive woman. Melody looks even younger than either of James's two daughters. Neither of them seems very happy with their dad's date, especially Debbie.

James starts introducing Melody to his family when all of his grandchildren start running up greeting him with, "Hi, Grandpa!" Also present is James's brother Sam, his wife Carol, their four daughters, three sons, and seventeen grandchildren. Mary's three sons are there with their wives and all of Mary's five grandchildren. The entire family is there for a family gathering. James continues his introduction of Melody to all of the family. Debbie is a bit sarcastic with the introduction by making remarks of, "I believe I know you. Melody, uh, where do you work?"

Melody's response is, "I am a high school teacher. I teach world history over at Calloway High School."

Debbie says, "Yes, I heard of it. Isn't it one of those intercity school?"

"It is within the confines of the city, so I guess you might say it is an intercity school."

James says to Debbie, "Yes, baby girl, she is an educator of teenagers, and we are on our way to get us a bite to eat. I am a bit hungry. Mr brother-in-law has prepared some good-looking food over here and we are about to dig in. I would suggest you do the same thing."

Music is playing prominently in the background, mostly musical choices of the younger family members. Everyone seems to be enjoying themselves.

Early the next morning, James is at the gym working hard on his physical condition as he always does when all at once, out of the corner of his eye, he sees his pastor and friend, Rev. Bledsoe, approaching with a smile and greetings of, "Good morning, Brother Lackey."

James returns the greeting. "Good morning, Pastor. I did not expect to see you here this morning."

The pastor says to James, "It is just as surprising to see you up this early in the morning."

"I usually try to get a little workout in the morning to get a good start on the day."

"Now that I have your ear. I have wanted to ask you for some time now. Have you seen sister Claudette Maddox lately? I only ask you this because I was beginning to get use to seeing the two of you together. The two of you make for fine-looking couple."

"You know, her son was seriously injured in an automobile accident, and I have not seen very much of her lately."

"I did hear about the accident. How is the young man doing?"

"I have not heard form Mrs. Maddox lately. I think she is taking her son's injury very hard."

"I placed a few calls to her and even spoke with her a few times, but now I get a disconnected phone message when I call. She seemed to be a bit preoccupied during the few times I was able to reach her. She did not seem to have much time for chitchat. She was once a very loyal and dedicated member of our church's congregation, and I would like very much for her to return to our congregation. I can go back many years and remember that she and her late husband were very good servants of the Lord."

"Yes, I know she is a fine woman, but I think her son's injury took its toll on her because it just seems that she is not interested in very much other than taking care of her son."

"Well I will let you get back to your morning workout. I am finished and on my way home, but if you happen to see her, let her know that the church doors are always open and our prayers will always include her and a speedy recovery for her son."

"Thank you, Pastor. I sure will and I will see you Sunday." Out of the corner of James's eye, rapidly approaching, James could see Karen Campbell.

She addresses James in a very sarcastic tone of voice. "Hello, Mr. Lackey, who are you f——king in this hole?"

James responds, "And a hello to you, Ms. Campbell. You are looking very beautiful today. Is this your regular workout location?"

"If it was, I would discontinue my membership."

"If not, it is the gym's loss." Karen just walks away from James without responding and leaves the gym. James is happy that this encounter was a mild one and did not lead to any kind of verbal confrontation. He then continues his workout.

CHAPTER

5

James's oldest daughter Pam Mills and her husband Joe along with their two kids arriving at the baseball park for a little league baseball game for Joe Jr., and to their surprise, Pam's dad James is also arriving. They meet in the parking area, and Little Joe is very excited to see his grandfather. He is especially happy to see his grandpa keeping his promise of attending some of his baseball games. James hugs his family, and they are all happy to see each other. Little Regina grabs her grandpa's hand and does not want to turn it loose. She is very happy to see her grandpa. Little Joe gathers his equipment as he explains to his grandpa that he has to hurry out to the playing field to warm up with his team mates, hugs his grandpa, and shakes his hand in excitement as he rushes out to be with his teammates. Joe Sr. Excuses himself also as he tells James that he has to go out and help Little Joe's coach with all of these future all-stars. James, Pam, and little Regina find their way to the bleachers to find a seat with all of the other family members. Pam is very happy to see her dad spending time with her family, gives him a big hug, and tells him how happy she is that he is spending this time with her family. James is now sitting and watching his grandson as he prepares for his upcoming game. Soon the game begins, and they are happily cheering for little Joe and his team. Little Joe is pitching for his team and is enjoying immediate success by getting three outs without giving up any runs. Once the game is over with, everyone is happy because Little Joe's team has won, and Little Joe rushes over to be with his grandpa. This is the day that Little Joe distribute the snacks to the teammates. Once the snack serving and playing are over, the family prepares to leave. James suggests that they all meet for a little pizza as a reward for Little Joe's team's win. Everyone agrees. Little Regina and Little Joe want to ride with their grandpa. Everyone agrees as they all get into their respective cars and departs for the pizza restaurant.

The family arrives at the restaurant for pizza and enters the restaurant to be seated. Everyone begins to order, but there is a little bit of disagreement between the kids over the toppings should be on the pizza. Everyone finally agrees on the toppings and places orders for two large pizzas with toppings to please all. As time passes, the kids are playing games with some kids that they have met in the pizza establishment and also a couple of Little Joe's teammates. There is much conversation between the adults. James is explaining to Peggy that his intentions are to make himself more available to his attention. James agrees because he knows that Debbie is much more demanding than Pam. Finally, they all agree that it is time everyone should be going home. Just as the family was about to leave, Karen Campbell enters the restaurant.

James is beginning to think, *How does she always know exactly where I am at? Maybe it is a coincidence because she cannot know my plans. Coming to this pizza restaurant was not planned. It just happened.*

Karen notices James and is very polite. "Hello, Mr. Lackey, introduce me. Are these your grandchildren that you are always talking about?

James not wanting his family to know anything about Karen attempts to make his conversation with Karen brief and out of range for them to hear, but Karen is determined to be involved and strikes up a conversation with Joe and the kids but ignores Pam. She introduces herself by saying, "Did you guys know that your grandfather and I have been dating. Who knows I just might become your new grandmother."

Peggy looking surprised asks her dad, "Who is this woman?"

James replies, "Just a woman out of my pass." Joe recognizes that maybe she is the woman form the office that everyone has been talking about. "They are all about to leave. I believe they have to be going."

Pam says, "Dad, I asked you once, and I am asking again, who is this woman?"

Joe tells Pam, "Maybe we should all leave. Kids, we are going. Come on, Pam." Pam finally decides to leave.

Karen says to James, "Well I can talk with you. Maybe you and I can enjoy a bite to eat, you know, just like old times."

James not wanting to get his family involved or getting Karen's temper tantrum going says, "I will join you for a bite to eat."

Pam returns and introduces herself. "Hi, my name is Pam. I am Mr. Lackey's daughter."

Joe not wanting this to go any further grabs Pam's hand and says, "We must be going, honey. This is Dad's guest. It was nice meeting you, Ms. Campbell." The family says good-bye to James and leaves for home.

James says to his family, "We need to do this more often. I mean get together as a family."

James and Karen are left alone. Karen says, "You can go. I have real friends joining me shortly."

James says, "It was good seeing you. I will be going now."

—m—

Couple of days later and James is on his way home form the office and decides to stop at the supermarket to pick up a few items for dinner, and while he is in the market shopping at the meat department, he feels a hand on his shoulder and hears, "Hello, stranger." As he turned around, to his surprise, it was Claudette Maddox. James and Claudette are both surprised to see each other. James has many questions that he wants to ask James. The two of them at the same time ask how each has been doing. They both laugh as each of them is asking the same question. James begins telling Claudette about the conversation that he had with Pastor Bledsoe about her not being at church lately, Claudette's response was that she has been spending her time taking care of Brad. James asks Claudette, "How is Brad?"

Claudette's response is, "You know, he suffered some major injures which is taking a bit of time for him to recover."

"My phone numbers are still the same. I can't say the same for you. I would like to see Brad and find out more about that accident and who was at fault."

"James, you know you and your firm do not handle automobile accidents."

"That is true but I can point him in the right direction. As a matter of fact, my son-in-law could probably be of some assistance to brad."

"Must I remind you, James, that Brad does not have much love for you. Brad feels I should stay as far away from you as possible."

"Is that what you want?"

"I guess it does not matter what I want. I just want Brad to have a full recovery."

"Are you totally happy with your life as the caretaker for your son? You must remember that I have a major stumbling block with one of my siblings also, so why don't you at least discuss the possibility of Brad speaking with my son-in-law."

"He needs to speak with someone because the only thing he is doing is talking about what he is going to do, and time is running out for him to do anything. He did speak with one or maybe two attorneys, but you know how difficult Brad can be sometimes and that relationship did not even get off the ground."

"Speak with Brad and get back with me. Maybe I can set something up for him. In the meantime, when are you going to have a little social time?"

Claudette smiles and says, "Maybe sooner than you think. I will get started by attending church services this Sunday. Maybe I can talk to Brad into coming along with me. We can start socializing together. In the meantime, Brad is home waiting on me to bring this." She points to ice cream in her basket that Brad ordered."

"You have been shopping for a bit more than ice cream."

Claudette has a full basket of groceries. Claudette leans over and gives James a hug and a kiss on the cheek. "This is it for now."

"Until Sunday. Remember, I said I am planning to attend church." She then leaves for the checkout line to go home. As James is returning to complete his shopping, he recognizes Karen Campbell with a shopping cart heading for Claudette.

James quickly cuts her direction and speaks, "Hello, Ms. Campbell."

"Is that one of your old b——s that you are f——king?"

"She is a very nice woman that attends the same church that I do."

"Even if she is, you are probably planning to f——king over her too."

"I guess you and I should just continue our shopping. This conversation will not lead to anything meaningful. Maybe you should find a church that you can embrace, with some nice people to make friends with."

James is hoping this encounter with Karen will end there. Karen does leave James to continue her shopping, but changes her mind, and is now following James around the store saying, "Are you going to talk with me? What's wrong, you can't talk now? I wonder if these good people know that you took me on a cruise and that you spent all of your time f——king me every morning, leading me on, and making promises. Now you don't want to speak with me. With you, it's f——'em and leave 'em."

James is trying to ignore her as he finishes his shopping. James heads for the checkout line with Karen following right behind him. He finally asks an employee if he could save his basket. He will have someone to pick it up for him. Karen follows James out to the parking lot. James is finally in his car driving away when Karen begins to throw whatever she could find at his car. James leaves the parking lot and heads for home, thinking that with all of the embarrassment that he just encountered, at least he has had a chance to see Claudette. Maybe there is hope for him and Claudette yet.

Claudette arrives home, and as expected, Brad was curious as to what had taken his mother so long at the supermarket. Claudette's explanation was, "The market was busy with long lines at the checkout, and as you can see, I purchased more than ice cream. We haven't been shopping for food lately, so I decided to purchase some food for the two of us to eat. By the way, I have not been attending church since your accident, and I think it is about time I attend church services. It might be a good idea for you to give some consideration to attending church also. You have much to be thankful for."

"Well, if you are considering going to church, maybe it will be good for me to go to church with my mama."

"Good, now that you have agreed to go to church with me this Sunday. I am going in and prepare you and I a good healthy dinner."

Brad smiles. "I guess this is the only way I am going to get dinner."

Claudette's response is, "You had better believe it, one other bit of business you need to take care of, and that is you have not spoken with your attorney lately about the accident."

"I don't have no attorney."

"Don't you think you should contact someone pretty soon? As you know, you have limits on the amount of time you can wait."

"Yes, Mother, I know. I will call somebody. What about that Mr. Lackey that you are all up in arms and busy seeing? He is a lawyer, isn't he?"

"Yes, and a very good one, but I don't think he handles these type cases."

"Well, he should at least be able to recommend a lawyer."

"He probably can, but I have always been led to believe that you don't care for Mr. Lackey."

"I don't when it comes to a relationship with my mama, but if he can use his contacts to get me some good legal representation, then business is business."

"I don't know if he is speaking to you and me anymore. You know how the two of us treated him, but if I see him, I will ask."

"Ah, Mom, you know you still have his number. Why don't you just call him?"

"Maybe I will try to call him tomorrow."

"Just don't think this is an opportunity for you to rekindle a romance."

"He is a very eligible, distinguished gentleman, and I am sure he has not been sitting around waiting for me."

"Well let's hope he's not."

—⚹—

James arrives home and suddenly remembers that he has committed to a house dinner date with his friend Melody Farrell. After a short period of time, his doorbell rings. As he opens the door, there is Melody with a smile, saying, "I hope you have everything for dinner because I did not bring anything and I am a lousy cook."

"We won't eat in. I didn't have time to prepare dinner, so I guess we will either be eating out or order take out, which do you prefer?"

Melody says, "That is your call. It doesn't matter to me."

"Let's eat out. You prefer Italian, I hope."

"Sound good to me. I love Italian."

"Italian it is. You know, I love Italian food."

"I believe you love all foods because wherever we go, you love the food."

James grins. "I guess I am not choosy. Feeding me has never been a major problem. A hot dog with mustard and onions and I am okay."

"Onions?" She frowns. "No kisses for you when you are eating hot dogs. I love the good old Chicago dog. Whenever I am in Chicago, I always have me a good old Chicago dog."

"I love the Chicago dog too, but that is when I visit Chicago." James then tells Melody that maybe they should leave for dinner even though there will not be any reservations for them.

Melody grabs James hand and says, "You lead and I will follow you to the eatery." James and Melody has arrived at the restaurant having dinner and enjoying themselves when all of a sudden, James observes Karen Campbell being seated at the next table to his table, but this time, she is with a man. James feels that her being with a man means that she won't be interested in him. Karen is seated and immediately introduces herself to James and his date. She introduces the man with her as her brother. Karen tells Melody and her brother that James and she have been dating in the pass.

She tells Melody, "You don't have anything to worry about, honey. It is over with us. You can have him. James took me on a beautiful cruise and f——ked me every morning before breakfast. Yes! We danced and partied all night and f——ked all morning. When we returned home, he was tired of f——king me and just dumped me."

"Ms. Campbell, Melody does not deserve this."

94

"I didn't deserve being just a good f—— either, but as I said, it is over between you and me."

Karen's brother says, "Come on, sis. Let's leave this man and woman alone."

James asks the waiter to bring his check. He also notices that Melody is not very happy. James pays his check and immediately leaves the restaurant.

———

During the drive home, all is very quiet until James notices that Melody is laughing out loud. James starts to laugh but is wondering why he is laughing and, more importantly, why is Melody laughing. Melody starts saying, "I have never seen the cool, calm James Lackey move that swiftly. How did you ever get involved with that job? Were you that hard up for sex?"

"I was impressed with a pretty face and body. That is why I dropped her for an even prettier face and body."

"You can cut out the bull crap. I do think you are very charming, and I only believe part of what she is saying."

"What part?"

"I am not saying you will have to guess."

"I guess I have been a little overworked and lonely for companionship."

"Just how many more women do you have angry at you after taking them on a cruise, dancing, and partying all night, and how should I say it, f——king every morning for breakfast? I guess I have been missing something. When am I going on a cruise?"

"I don't like you like that, but we can take a cruise if you think that will satisfy you."

Melody laughs. "What about f——king me for breakfast every morning?"

"We can start the latter just as soon as we reach my house."
"That is a promise." She makes a little wink. "I am going to hold you to your word."

—⚍—

Sunday morning, there was rain and it had been very windy. The wind had blown down power lines, trees as a matter of fact. It was quite a storm. Claudette is busy getting ready for church anyway, and Brad seems to be happy also as he is preparing to go to church for the first time in recent memories, wishing he had invited Diana to go along with them. The two finish preparing themselves for church and head for the garage to get into the minivan but find out that here is a tree down across the exit from the garage and they could not get the van out of the garage. The two of them return to the house where Claudette places a call to her daughter Peggy, but there is no answer. She then places a call too her son Pearce, but as expected, there is no answer. She realizes that she and Brad are stranded, and her promise to James will go unfulfilled again.

—⚍—

James arrives at church with much anticipation, even though the weather is wet and windy. He parks his car, enters the church, and notices that most of the congregation is absent due to weather. There is hope that Claudette would not be one of the absent congregation members, but after a while, James realizes that Claudette probably would not be attending services this Sunday, so he just enjoys Rev. Bledsoe's sermon. After the services has concluded, James notices that Rev. Bledsoe motioning him to wait as if though the pastor has something to say. James slowly walks over to the reverend who is surrounded by members of the congregation talking to him. James has stood silently until he hears the reverend say, "Excuse me, ladies. I want to speak with Brother Lackey about Sister Claudette Maddox."

One lady says, "How is she? Has anyone seen her or her son since the accident?"

The minister says, "That is what I want to speak with Brother Lackey about." The minister turns to James and asks, "How are you today, brother?"

James says, "I am fine, Pastor, and I did have a chance to speak with Sister Maddox a few days ago. She indicated to me that she would see me today for church services, but I guess because of the weather and all, she was unable to attend."

Pastor says, "We had a lot of people absent today. I guess we can blame the weather and realize that God's reason for making it possible for only the few of us to attend services today was God's will." James agrees with the reverend and tells the reverend that he feels that Sister Claudette is doing much better these days." Her son Brad is much improved and maybe she will attend next Sunday, maybe Brad will be able to attend with her."

The pastor says, "We hope so! We will continue our prayers for both of them."

"Yes, Pastor, we will." He excuses himself by thanking the pastor for the sermon he delivered as he departs for home.

Claudette and Brad are home waiting for the tree to be removed from the front of their garage door. They are happy that their home did not receive any damage from the storm. Brad is telling Claudette that maybe he could use a bite to eat and says that he is sorry for not being able to attend church services today. He says, "You know, it has been a long time since I have attended church of any kind."

Claudette replies, "I was really looking forward to hearing Rev. Bledsoe's sermon this morning too. I will fix us a little something to eat."

"Maybe next Sunday, but in the meantime, I am going to watch the game."

Claudette begins preparing some food for the two of them and, at the same time, wondering what could James be thinking of her not showing up for church today. Perhaps she is not reliable. Brad is flipping through TV channels to watch the football game.

CHAPTER

6

Brad and Claudette arrive at the parking lot to Brad's doctor's office when they observe a lot of police officers surrounding the entrance to the building. Brad says, "What the—" He then looks at his Mom. "Sorry, Mama."

Claudette says, "You had better watch your mouth around me."

A policeman walks over to the car and says, "If you people are seeking entrance to this building, I am sorry to say that no one is allowed in this building at this time."

Claudette says, "Officer, would I be out of line if I asked why? Because we have a doctor's appointment today."

The officer says, "I am sorry, miss. I guess you can reschedule," "What is wrong?"

The officer says, "There was a crime committed here today, and this entire building is a crime scene until further notice."

Claudette asked the Officer if he could at least let them know what the crime was and how serious. The officer says, "The bank was robbed. That is all I can tell you, and I would suggest that the two of you move along to some place else."

Claudette says, "Well, Brad, I guess we had better return home." They prepare to leave and exit the location. They start driving down the street home. They stop at a light. A young man walks over to their car and requests that they open the door, but they refuse. At this time, the young man produces a gun and orders them to open the door. Claudette unlocks the door. The young man quickly enters the van.

A frightened young man sits in the backseat of the van and says, "Let's get out of here."

Claudette says, "What do you mean get of here?"

The young man says, "Let's go home."

Claudette says, "What home?"

He says, "To your house."

Brad asks, "What is your name, man?"

His response is, "You do not need to know my name. Just drive." Claudette starts to drive. The young man says, "To your house. I hope you live in a nice house with an attached garage. Let me see some identification with your address on it." He reaches into the front seat and grabs Claudette's purse and starts looking through her purse.

Brad says, "Man, you had better put my mother's purse down. The young man responds by pointing the gun at Brad and saying, "You must forget who has the gun?"

Brad says, "You had better be glad that you do have the gun. Even with all mu injury problems—"

Claudette interrupts, "Let him go through the purse, son."

The young man says, "Good, just listen to your mama, boy." He locates Claudette's driver's license, and says, "Now let's go home to your house. That is a pretty fancy neighborhood where you live in. It just might be a nice place to get a new car to travel in, maybe this van." Brad is still not happy and realizes with all of his injuries that there is not very much he can do, so he just prepares himself for the ride home when all of a sudden, Brad recognizes the same police officer from the robbery scene driving the same direction as he and his mom. They stop for the light. Claudette positions her van in such a way that it blocks the path of the police car. The officer jumps out of his squad car a bit agitated because of the position of the van blocking his pathway, and as he slowly approaches the van, the officer orders everyone out of the van, but the bank robber orders Claudette to drive on as fast as she can. The officer runs back to his squad car and starts to pursue the van. The young bank robber is giving orders to both Claudette and Brad that they had better not blow this one. The police officer is following the van and calling for help. Claudette is driving in such a way that is obvious that she was hoping to be caught. The young man takes his jacket off, and Brad notices that he is wearing a name tag with the name Bob on it. At which time, he says Bob and the young man looks up at Brad and says, "Where do you know my name from?"

Brad says, "It is right there on your shirt."

Bob says, "Oh!"

Claudette continues to drive, and she tells Bob, "We won't be able to travel very long because I only have about a half tank of gas."

Bob says, "We will drive as long as we can until I figure something out."

Claudette continues to drive, and as she approaches a freeway, Bob instructs her to take the freeway. Claudette proceeds to enter the freeway with the police in pursuit. At this time, there are other police cars chasing and helicopters flying above. Bob begins to get nervous and starts screaming, "Can't you drive this thing faster?"

Claudette says, "This is all I have. We cannot drive any faster."

After driving for a while with all the of police escort and the news media also flying above helicopters, the van is now running on low gas. Bob realizes that the gas is running out, and he thinks about running but realizes that he will not get very far, so he decides that he has two hostages and will take advantage of the situation he has created. Claudette finally has to pull the van to a stop in the middle of the freeway all of the police cars pulls up to the rear and begin to exit their vehicles with guns drawn and barks out orders for the occupants to exit with their hands up one at a time, but no one inside of the van moved as Bob is giving orders inside for Claudette and Brad to stay put at which time Bob yells out of the van to the officers that he has a gun and two hostages. He will be giving the orders or they will have two dead bodies in the van. At this time, the police have the freeway traffic blocked in both directions. No cars can move in either direction. Bob tells Claudette and Brad that they had better do as he says or all three of them are going to end up dead. The police has run a check on the van and finds out that it is registered to a Mrs. Claudette Maddox. One officer yells Claudette's name and asks if she is okay and Claudette responds that she is okay but scared and that her son has limitations from recent automobile accident that he was in.

Bob yells out that unless he is allowed out of this situation, he is prepared to die and will take his two hostages with him. The hostage situation continues for the remainder of the day and into the night with the freeway closed to all traffic in both directions with police officers trying to develop ways to rescue Claudette and Brad. Bob is now becoming more and more demanding to the police by making such statements as, "I have given you police long enough to bring me another vehicle full of gas and transportation by plane out of this city."

A police officer identifies herself as Captain Sandra Evans, speaks to Bob saying, "We are trying to secure the necessary means for you to get out of town, but we want you to release the hostages unharmed."

Bob says, "You must think I am bit crazy by releasing my two new friends without a guarantee out of this city. Now bring me a car with a full tank of gas with no police escort, and I promise you I will release both of them unharmed once I am in the clear. They will have my permission to call you with their location once I am far enough away."

Captain Evans in her attempt to continue stalling Bob asks, "What about the plane?"

Bob responds, "Forget the d——n plane. Just get me a car with a full tank of gas, and now I want money. How about fifty grand as spending change? You know I will need a few extra bucks to live on once I am free."

Captain Evans says, "What about the money you already have?"

Bob says, "I didn't get very much. I will need more to live on. Better still just shut the f—— up and do as I say. I am tired of negotiating with you. I am giving you one more hour and then either I have the car and money or all three of us will die and as many of you as I can take down with me will also die, so let's quit talking and get to work."

Captain Evans begins discussing the situation with her fellow officers. "Where is this d——n squad of marksmen that I ordered hours ago?"

One officer responds finally, "They are on their way. They should be here shortly."

Captain Evans says, "I hope so because this guy is crazy. I believe he will do as he says."

At this time, an officer identifies himself as Captain Oleander reporting as commander of the Special Recondo Squad, an alert police squad that was developed by Captain Oleander, specializing in situation involving hostage situations. "We can get this guy, and we won't harm his hostages. We have night vision that will allow my marksman to pinpoint the suspect. How many people are in the car?"

Captain Evans responds, "there are three—the bank robber suspect, an elderly woman around sixty years old, and her son who is somewhat handicapped."

Captain Oleander informs Captain Evans that being that it is nighttime, the police will have to use the night vision with scopes on their weapons. He explains to Captain Evans the procedure that this men and women will be using. Captain Oleander explains to Captain Evans how perfect the members in this unit have to be with a rifle and how they will set up to take this person out with one shot. Captain Evans says, "Let's get this show on the road. I have been waiting long enough, and I believe this person will do what he has been saying he will do."

Captain Oleander instructs the unit to position themselves for action, and the identity of the suspect reminds them that this has to work because a woman and her son's life are at stake. As the Recondos prepare for action, Captain Evans begins thinking that if this doesn't work, two innocent lives will be lost. At this time, she hears a rifle shot and the announcement that it is all over. Once confirmed that the suspect was dead, Captain Evans rushes to the van to find out if the two hostages are okay and they are. Captain Evans identifies herself, and she identifies Captain Oleander to Claudette and Brad. Captain Evans instructs the paramedics to find out how Claudette and Brad are doing and gives instructions for the area to be prepared for the arrival of the corner, knowing that this freeway will continue to be shutdown until there is a complete investigation of everything that has taken place here today and the body has been removed.

Claudette and Brad are taken to the hospital emergency to be checked out, and at the same time, Claudette and Brad are busy placing phone calls to their family to let them know that they are okay and also finding out that there has been wall-to-wall television news coverage of them being held hostages. Diana is telling Brad just how worried they all have been about him and his mom and that she will be at the house waiting for them to get home. "As a matter of fact, I think your sister, brother, and your entire family will be here waiting. I think Peggy has a key to the house." A few hours passes, Brad and Claudette are found to have survived this ordeal relatively well and is released from the hospital. They find captain Evans waiting for them, telling both of them that she wants them to go home and get some rest because there are many questions that has to be answered before this investigation can be completed. She also informed them that there is some news media that will want to interview both of them, but they don't have to answer any questions, unless they want too. "As a matter of fact, we have car waiting to take you guys home." Captain Evans also advised them that their van is is police custody for evidence.

Claudette says, "Well I guess we will just have to find other means of transportation until we get our van back."

Captain Evans tells them that they should have their van returned by day's end. Claudette and Brad thank the captain as they leave.

—⚅—

Claudette and Brad arrive home, and it is beginning of daybreak. They observe that all of their family is there waiting for them, except for Diana. Claudette observes that her cell phone has not been turned on lately, and she has several messages form James. She wants to return his calls after listening to his message informing her that he is aware of her ordeal and wants to know if she and Brad are all right. Claudette decides that she would rather return James's calls in privacy, so she waited until she has let her family see for themselves that she and Brad are okay and she is alone in her bedroom. Everyone is showing happiness in Claudette's house. All of her children and their families have all been waiting for her and Brad. After the greetings and welcoming, they are preparing breakfast for everyone. Brad says, "Mom and I thank you guys very much for being here, but we are very tired, and if you could excuse us, at least me, I am going to get some rest."

Claudette says, "I am very tired also. It has been a long day and a long night. I need some sleep. Thanks for being here. I love you all. You can stick around but be quiet while I sleep."

Claudette's son Pearce says, "Mom, we are going to let you and Brad get some rest, We will go out and have some breakfast. The kids need to get ready for school, and we will come back and visit you later."

Jim Olsen says, "Come on, everybody. Let's get out of here and let Mom and Brad get some rest." Everybody leave Claudette's house. Claudette goes into her room to place a call to James.

—⚅—

Claudette enters her bedroom and quickly places a call to James's cell phone but no answer. She leaves a message, so she places a call to his home phone but still no answer, and again she leaves a message. Finally she decides to call James's office where she is expecting to hear the voice of Mary Winfield, the longtime assistant to James but found out that Mary was out of the office serving jury duty, so she leaves a message for James at his office. Claudette soon falls asleep, hoping that James would get at least one of her messages.

Late morning, James is out of town on business and is checking into his hotel but decides to go check in at the office by checking his box for messages and is hoping that he would find a message from Claudette. There was no message, so he decides to call his office to speak with Mary for an update on his messages and realizes that Mary is out of the office serving jury duty. He asks for his messages anyway. Mary's replacement is on a break, and he is not able to speak with that person, so James continues to check into the hotel. Once he reaches his room, he discovers that he has several messages on his phone, and one of the messages is from Claudette, so James quickly calls Claudette but there is no answer. Claudette is asleep and does not hear the phone. James leaves a message for Claudette that he is out of town on business. James has a meeting scheduled, so he proceeds to get dressed for his meeting that he is sure would take up most of his day.

Later in the day, Claudette is finally awake, checks her messages, and finds out that she did receive a call from James.

She makes an attempt to return James's call, but again, she is unable to do so because James is in a meeting and does not answer his phone. The day is passing, and Claudette decides to place another phone call to James, and again she only gets his voice mail, so Claudette suddenly decides that she will try to send James a text message. Claudette has never placed a text before and is not sure that she knows how to send a text. She decides to try it anyway. She makes a text attempt and find out that her phone is not set up for texting, so she decides to ask Brad if he knows anything about texting. Brad said he does, because he sends text messages all the time. Claudette tells Brad that her phone is not set up for texting. Brad points out to her that her phone is a little old, but she could send a text if she wants. Brad proceeds to point out the difference in his phone that he uses for texting on a regular basis and Claudette's phone. Brad tells Claudette that she could use his phone to send a text message, but Claudette decides against using Brad's phone because she did not want Brad to know that she was sending message to James. Claudette asks Brad if he is hungry, and Brad says, "I guess it is about time I had a little food. It has been awhile since my last meal."

Claudette says, "Good, I am hungry. Maybe I will fix us a bite to eat. I think the gang will be back to visit us just as soon as they are all off from work and the kids are home form school."

Later in the day, the doorbell rings. Claudette goes to door, opens it, and finds out that it is Brad's girlfriend Diana. Diana and Claudette greet each other with pleasant exchanges and says, "Where is he?"

Claudette says, "Right in front of the TV."

Diana proceeds to Brad and gives him a hug. Brad is glad to see her, especially since he has not seen her since before the big ordeal. Claudette proceeds to the kitchen to begin preparing some food for Brad and her. She hollows out to Diana that she is preparing some food for her and Brad and asks Diana if she would like some food. Diana responds with, "No, I am not hungry."

The day is ending. Brad and Diana are still making out like two lovebirds. Claudette still has not heard form James. She will not call anymore today. Maybe something is wrong or maybe he just feels that after all of his calls earlier with no return, maybe she is avoiding him again. Claudette is not giving up so easy this time and will call James tomorrow morning.

Early the following morning, James is in the hotel restaurant having breakfast with couple of the people that he was in town to meet with when his cell phone rings. James answers. It is Claudette, so James excuses himself form the table to talk with Claudette. The two of them start explaining to each other how they have been missing each other. James tells Claudette that he will have to cut his phone call short, but he will be back in town tonight and feels that the two of them should get together. Claudette agrees. James returns to the table with a big smile on his face, which is detected by his breakfast guests. One of them says with a smile, "That must have been some good news."

"Believe me, it was." He returns to complete his breakfast, very much looking forward to getting home and getting together with Claudette.

—⚏—

Later in the day around sundown, James arrives back in town goes to pick up his car. He only has carry-on baggage and no checked baggage. The drive home takes a little longer than James has planned, due to the time of day, which is during rush hour. There is also a stalled car on the freeway. James finally arrives home and finds his daughter Pam driving into his driveway behind him. Pam says, "I guess you are surprised to see me. I did not think you were home. I just wanted to pay a visit to see my daddy. Due to your busy schedule, I don't see much of you anymore, and I just wanted to come by and pay you a visit. I tried calling you at the office earlier today but was told that you were out of town on business and scheduled to return this afternoon."

James hugs Pam and says, "I guess I will have to start keeping my word by spending more time with you and your family as promised. I am going do the same for Deb. I an just now arriving home from an overnight trip out of tow, which Joe probably has already told you about. Come on in the house and let's talk."

James notices that Pam is not her usual self and seems a bit concerned about something. James asks the question, "What is wrong with my little girl?"

Pam responds, "Daddy, I am not a little girl anymore."

James says, "You will always be my little girl."

Pam squeezes her Dad's hand and puts her arm around his waist as the two of them enters the house. James once again asks Pam what is wrong. "Tell Dad. It is my job to solve my girls' problems."

Pam asks her Dad to have a seat as she attempts to tell him her problems. "Daddy, you know Joe and I have been married for over twelve years now."

James looks at Pam and says, "Yes, twelve years, it has been twelve years and you guys have presented me with two wonderful grandchildren. I am very proud to call Joe one of my sons that I never had."

Pam says, "Well, Dad, I am not sure our marriage is very good anymore."

James says, "Is there something that I don't know about? You know I see Joe every day every day when I go to work, and he seems to be happy while at work.

Pam says, "You know, we are arguing more and more these days, and most of the time, we argue over small silly things."

James wants to place a call to Claudette as promised, but he also knows that his daughter needs him now, so he starts asking her if she suspects another woman, and Pam's says, "I don't believe he is cheating because I always know where he is and he treats the kids well."

James says, "I repeat myself, Well what is wrong?"

Pam says, "I think he is getting tired of me. I don't think I am attractive to him anymore."

James says, "When he is at work, his conversation is always inclusive of you and the kids I just know he loves you more today than he ever did. Do you and him ever sit down and have that conversation?"

Pam says, "we don't talk very much most of the time when he comes home. We have dinner and supervise the kids during their homework and off to bed to rest for the next day."

James says, "I bet I know what will solve you guys' problem——some together time without the kids, so I am going to tell you what I am going to do. There is this little romantic place where your mom and I use to spend quality time. I just know you guys will enjoy, so just plan on Joe Jr., Regina and I spending the weekend together, and I will have Mary form my office make the reservations. You and Joe will have a weekend on your dad."

Pam smiles and looks at her Dad and says, "You will do that for me?"

James replies, "For my little girl, the world."

Pam hugs her dad and says, "Maybe this is all we need. Daddy, I am going get out of your hair and go home to my husband and kids."

To which James says, "Just leave everything up to Daddy. I will see Joe tomorrow at the office. Don't tell him anything. I will tell him that this is an early anniversary gift to you guys."

Pam hugs her dad again and says, "Thank you, Daddy. Now you know why I love you so much. This just might work. I will see you this weekend when you check in for babysitting duties. The kids will be happy to spend the weekend with Grandpa." Pam leaves for home. James immediately places a call to Claudette but received no answer at her house, so he decides to try her cell phone but there still is no answer. So he leaves a message that he called and that he is a bit hungry so he will be at the restaurant that the two of them usually meet at having dinner.

James is having dinner alone when he observes Claudette and Brad headed toward his table. James stands, welcomes the two of them, and is surprised to see Bran greeting him with a smile. Claudette is also surprised to see the response of Brad. Brad shakes James's hand. Claudette greets James with a hug and slightly kisses him on the cheek. The two of them take a seat at James's request and start conversing with each other. James asks the waiter to bring two more menus and informs him that it will now be three for dinner. All is quiet as Claudette and Bran is seated. After they have all read the menu, they order their meals, and finally Claudette says to James, "So how have you been?"

"I can't complain, just a little busy." After a short time, the drinks are being delivered to the table. After a bit more conversation without Brad being involved, dinner is served. Finally Brad decides to speak and inquire of James the possibilities of some legal advice on his accident and what rights he has.

James, a little surprised, says, "Hello, Brad!"

Brad responds, "Hello, Mr. Lackey!"

James says, "I can answer your question." He then tells Brad that he will have someone contact him tomorrow with answers and is much more familiar with what kind of representation he will need. Brad seems to be happy with the answer and says that he will wait for the phone call. Brad is now involving himself in the table conversation. The three of them continue in conversation y debating the possibilities of having dessert and coffee. Finally Brad decides to order a very large desert. James and Claudette pass on desert and order coffee. The evening ends with everyone smiling and having good time. The three of them are now the only customers left in the restaurant, so they decide that it is time to pay the check and head for home. James wanted to spend the night with Claudette but decides to leave well enough alone and head for home.

Chapter

7

James is busy getting dressed for a day's work when his phone rings, and it is Claudette calling James to tell him how much she enjoyed their brief meeting for dinner the previous night. She also tells him that she thinks Brad also enjoyed himself and is looking forward to meeting the attorney that James is referring him to. James tells Claudette that he will have his son-in-law, Joe Mills, contact Brad later today. Joe is a very good attorney and will do a good job for Brad. James tells Claudette that he is also happy about the dinner meeting last night. "Who knows? Maybe this one dinner meeting just might lead to future dinners, and future dinners could eventually lead to something meaningful again. Maybe a relationship continuing just where we left off."

Claudette jokingly says, "You and I are both feeling out oats today, and you just might be right. Well I don't want to make you late. I know you must have a busy day ahead of you. I just wanted to let you know that last night was fun."

"Thanks, I really do have a long and busy day waiting for me. I will get in touch with you later today and give Brad my message. Let him know that I enjoyed talking with him and maybe we can do it again real soon.

—m—

Upon James's arrival for work, he observed that something out of the ordinary is taking place in the building that houses his office. There are lots of police activity, and there is also activity by the fire department. James is thinking that maybe the building is on file, but there is no smoke or evidence of a fire, so he decides to park and join the commotion. Then he suddenly realizes that all of the staff from his office is outside on the sidewalk. James starts asking questions and finds out that a young woman with a gun is occupying his office.

All of a sudden, Mary Winfield is approaching James at a rapid pace and tells James, "She came up looking for you this morning, and this time, she has a gun."

James wants to know who came up looking for him this morning. "Who is up there?"

Mary's response is, "That Karen Campbell lady that came up before." This is not the news James is prepared for this morning.

Mary informs James, "That Karen came in this morning right after the office opened and stated that you and her will be getting married today and she will be waiting in your office. I did not want to allow her in your office. She just walked in without permission, so I decided to call you, but before I could contact you, she came out with two guns now, one in each hand, telling me that she is still waiting and you are not there. She is not waiting all day. I waiting for her to return to your office and lose the door. Immediately called the police and informed everyone in the office what is happening and insisted that we all leave and let the police handle it."

"You did the right thing!" James approaches a policeman to inquire about the person occupying his office.

The police officer says, "We have been looking forward to meet you. Yes, there is an armed woman in your office demanding to see you. She is telling everyone that the two of you are getting married today, and she will only leave when you get there to pick her up."

James asks the officer if he thinks it would do any good for him to try to speak with the woman. The officer tells James, "The decision what to do is not mine, but I will take you to the right person."

The officer takes James to his commanding officer, Captain Bentley, The captain told James, "Maybe you won't have to do anything. She has surrendered. She will be out shortly, but I would like for you to remain here with us. We would like to ask you a few questions about this woman."

There is news media stationed at the scene and is trying to ask James questions. James is not interested in answering any questions and refers them to his son-in-law. James remains with the police department to answer questions. Soon, two police officers exit the building, one on each side of Karen that is now wearing handcuffs. Captain Bentley asked James if he can make himself available for any information that he has pertaining to Miss Campbell. James tells Captain Bentley that he is available whenever he is needed.

Two days later, James finds out that Karen Campbell is being released on bond. James immediately asks his attorney to secure a restraining order against Karen. That if possible will order Karen to not come closer than one hundred yard of James, his office, or home. James is not sure Karen will honor this order, but he wants it anyway. The general feeling is that Karen needs expert help from the appropriate doctor.

—∿—

It is Sunday morning, and James remains a bit rattled about what happened in his office and is wondering if Claudette has found out about it. As he arrives for church services, he observed Claudette and Brad already seated in the church. James also sees that a seat is close behind them and immediately takes that seat. He makes sue that Claudette noticed that he is also in church. Claudette and Brad both acknowledge James. The services are starting to take place with opening proceedings taking place. They all are anticipating an enthusiastic message from Pastor Bledsoe. Finally Pastor Bledsoe begins his presentation, and his sermon is everything and more that they are expecting. Once the services has concluded, they begin to exit the church when James recognizes his daughter Debbie standing at the rear of the church talking to some other members of the congregation. James walks over to speak with her, and Debbie says, "Hi, Daddy, I didn't know you were here."

James says, "Well you should know why by now that I am usually here every Sunday, but the surprise is my seeing you here. You remember Ms. Maddox, and this is her son Brad Maddox."

Debbie is not happy to see James and Claudette exiting the church together, and her facial expressions expresses just how she is feeling about this occurrence.

Claudette says, "Hi, darling, my son and I happened to meet your dad in church this morning and we were about to head home."

James interrupts and says, "Why don't we all go over to the neighborhood café and have a late breakfast."

117

Debbie says, "I cannot go, I promised Frank and the girls that I would meet them immediately after church. We are shopping for ma a new car."

James says, "Well if you have to go, you have to go."

Debbie says, "Daddy, I will call you later," and then leaves.

James looks at Claudette and Brad and says, "I guess the three of us can go have a bite."

Brad says, "I can't stay either, I have a date with Ms. Diana Woods."

Claudette says, "Well you can count me in. I am ready to go, but I guess I will have to drop Brad off. Brad, where are you meeting Dianna at this time?"

Brad says, "Right here," as Diana walks up and starts to speak to everyone. James is wondering if any one of them has found out about his most recent encounter with Karen Campbell. There is no mentioning of the event during the greetings. Claudette and James bid a good-bye to Diana and Brad. James and Claudette are stuck with two cars. Brad realizes that his mom has her car and suggests to her, "We are going close to home and I can drop mom's car at the house."

Claudette says, "One problem, Brad, you know you can't drive."

To which Brad responds, "I have been driving, and if you don't believe, ask Diana."

Diana says, "Yes, Mrs. Maddox. He has been driving and he is driving normal. He wanted to surprise you."

Claudette says, "I am surprised!"

Brad says, "Mom, just go and enjoy your late breakfast or lunch, whichever you are having."

Claudette says, "Well call me after you drop the car off."

Brad says, "Don't worry, Momma," and departs for the van.

James and Claudette are about to head for James's car just when the two of them heard the voice of Pastor Bledsoe saying, "Sister Maddox, I am glad to see you in church today. It has been a while."

Claudette says, "Well, Pastor, you know my youngest son Brad was injured very bad in an automobile accident, but now he is much better and I wouldn't be surprised if you see a lot more of me around here."

Pastor Bledsoe says, "We will be looking forward to it." After a few more minutes of conversation, James and Claudette depart for the car and head for the restaurant.

—⁂—

Monday morning, James is busy at work in his office when his executive assistant, Mary Winfield, says, "Mr. Lackey, you have a visitor."

As James looks up, there was his daughter Debbie standing there with her arms extended for a hug, saying, "Daddy, you should be glad to see your youngest daughter,"

To which James replies, "What did I do to deserve this pleasure?"

Debbie replies, "I told you yesterday that I would call, but I figured you would appreciate the conversation with a live body and the live body being me."

James says, "Well, that is so important that you took time out of your daily routines to spend this unannounced visit with your papa? Why don't we just have a seat?"

Debbie proceeds to sit and begins by saying, "Daddy, I thought you and that Ms. Maddox were no longer seeing each other, but I must admit at least she is close to your age. That is more than I can say about all those other bimbos you have been seen with lately."

James laughs. "Bimbos'? Is that what you think of your daddy's friends? Mrs. Maddox is a fine woman, and we enjoy each other's company. We have a lot in common with each other. You know, we lost your mother a little over two years ago, and she lost her husband a short time before that. We are both getting older and lonely. I am tired of running around trying to act like an immature wannabe."

Debbie replied, "Daddy, you know how I feel, and I think most of it is I still miss my momma. I spoke with Pam about you and Mrs. Maddox. Pam tells me that I should mind my own business. She says you are an adult and can make up your own mind about what your life is going to be and I should just allow you to be Daddy and as Daddy just get on with your life."

James says, "We both miss Mom and anything I do will always be done with respect for my love of Margie, which means I have no plans of doing anything that I think will disrespect your mom. Your mom was my first love, and I really did love that woman and will never forget her."

Debbie says, "I know, Daddy, I know you and Momma loved each other. I was there with you and had to relive the pain along with you. I just want you too be happy, and if Mrs. Maddox solves that problem, well maybe I should not be so selfish and maybe both of you can have a little happiness, so from now on, you will not have any more problems from me." She hugs her daddy. "I will have a few questions about a woman announcing to the world that you and her are supposed to get married. That will have to be another time. I am going to let you get back to work. I am sure you have a lot more to do than sit around talking to me."

James says, "Did you get the new car?"

Debbie says, "We sure did. The girls and me will be over when you have time and take you for a ride."

James says, "I will be looking forward to it."

Debbie says, "Daddy, I love you, and I am so happy to have a father that understands that sometimes his little girls are not always grounded no matter if they seem to be all grown up. They will still need that Daddy comfort better known as live and understanding. I must go now." She hugs James, and they say bye as Debbie leaves.

As the week passes, James is seen with Debbie as they pick the girls up from school. Debbie, James, and Debbie's two little girls are taking a ride in Debbie's new SUV. James asks the girls what would they like to do, and they tell James that they would like to take a ride down by the ocean and buy some ice cream."

Debbie says, "No problem with me, Just remember that there is homework."

The girls answer, "We know!" They soon arrive at the ocean and find a very busy little place what advertises many flavors of ice cream. The four of them quickly get in line to purchase ice cream. They purchase the ice cream and find a seat to eat their ice cream. The girls meet another little girl their ages who happens to be with her mom and dad. The girls begin to play with their new friend. James and Debbie sit and become briefly engaged in conversation with the little girl's parents, which is as the little girl's parents has to leave and take their little girl with them. James and Debbie start a conversation about James's relationship with Karen Campbell. The children continue to play without their new friend. James and Debbie's conversation transitions into the subject that

Debbie is very serious about. Debbie informs James that she has a doctor's appointment coming up that she is nervous about. Debbie tells James that she had a mammogram and the doctor wants to run some further tests.

Debbie reminds her dad that her mom's history with breast cancer is the cause for her to check herself. "Even at my young age, I am worried that I won't see Laura and Christina grow up. I have not told Frank."

James says, "You mean he doesn't know?"

Debbie says, "I am afraid. You are the only person I have told. I have not even told Pam."

James hugs his daughter and says, "I am confident that you are going to be okay, but you had better let Frank know something. You know he deserved to know."

Debbie says, "I plan to let Frank know when he gets home. He is busy enjoying a day off from work, and he is playing golf with a few of his coworkers in an employee golf tournament."

"Do you need me to go with you to the doctor's office?"

Debbie says, "I want frank with me, but I just wanted you to know first because you were there for Mom."

James replies, "We didn't know anything was wrong with your mom until it was too late. It sounds like your condition has been diagnosed early."

Debbie says, "The doctor tells me that if there is a problem, she believes we caught it early." Debbie knows that the time for her and the girls to start heading home has arrived. "I guess me and the girls should be getting home because that golf game is probably over with pretty soon, and Fran will be looking for his girls as he like to say."

Debbie tells the girls, "Well we have better be going before Daddy gets home and wonders where we are. "They all get into Debbie's new car and head for home. James tells Debbie to keep him informed.

Debbie says, "You know I will!"

―∿―

Debbie and the girls drop James off at his home and soon arrive home. She tells the girls that they can play while she prepares dinner. At the same time, Debbie is trying to figure a way to let Frank know about her problem. She does not know how Frank will take the news. Debbie decides to call her sister Pam. Pam answers the phone, and Debbie's first question is, "What time are you expecting Joe home from the office?"

Pam's response is, "Well, you know, Joe tells me that he is making a stop with a client. You know how Joe is when he is meeting with a client. He will wait until he is hungry and full of beer or something and then come home looking for food. Maybe I should get him to take me and the kids out for dinner."

Debbie says, "Well if you guys don't have any plans, why don't you guys come over and I will do the cooking. I can fire up the old grill."

Pam says, "That sounds like a good idea, but the kids have unfinished homework. I will let you know as soon as Joe gets home."

Debbie says, "I will get Frank warmed up to do the cooking. You know he thinks he is the world's greatest when it comes to grilling food."

Pam says, "I thought you said you were going to do the cooking."

Debbie jokingly says, "I am doing the cooking, but I have an executive assistant by the name of Frank Samuels."

Pam says, "I will call you when Joe gets home and the kids finish their homework."

Debbie says, "I will be waiting, big sis." Debbie says bye and hangs the phone up. Then quickly places a call to Frank.

Frank answers the phone. "Hello, sweetheart."

Debbie says, "Hi, darling, I was wondering if you could pick up some steaks on your way home. I want enough for two families, and the families are my big sister's and yours. We are having a dinner party tonight."

Frank says, "What brought on the unexpected dinner party? And you must have forgotten that tomorrow is a school day."

Debbie replies, "No, I have not forgotten. I know that tomorrow is a school day. I just feel like my big sister and I should get our families together, and maybe we should even go to church with Dad this Sunday." Frank begins to wonder what is going on but asks no questions and agreed to pick up the meat.

—⧑—

Frank arrived home with the meat. Debbie is on the phone with Pam to fins that approximate time that she, Joe, and the children are planning on arriving. Debbie and Pam end the phone call and hang up as Frank comes over to Debbie and give her a hug and kiss. The girls come into the room to greet their Dad. Debbie tells Frank that she wants to speak with him before the arrival of her sister and her family. Frank starts to think that something is wrong and excuses the girls to go back play and finish their homework as he asked Debbie to explain what is wrong. Debbie says, "It is probably nothing that you are thinking. I want you to sit down."

Frank sits and says, "What is wrong? Then let me know. It is not any member of my family, my mom, my brother, or my sister is it?"

Debbie says, "It is nothing like that. It is that you know how my mother dies and all, so I decided to pay a visit to my doctor to request a mammogram and the results has some questions. The doctor wants to see me Tuesday. She tells me that I should not worry, but I can't help it. Now you know my reason for having my sister over. She doesn't know anything, but I plan to tell her tonight."

Frank hugs Debbie and says, "You know I will have to be strong for you and encourage you to not give up. Let us pray on it. I know the Lord will pull us through this little bump in the road."

Debbie says, "I am not giving up. The doctor told me that there is no evidence of anything wrong. It is that she saw something and wants to make sure it is not anything to be worried about. You know I am going to worry anyway. Oh, the doctor also said that if, I mean if she finds anything positive, I did a good thing by coming in for test now, especially with Mom's history."

Frank says, "I don't know much about breast cancer but you can bet I will know something next week."

Debbie says, "The doctor says that if there are some positive results and we catch it early, the survival rate is very good.

Frank continues to hug Debbie and says, "I will be there with you every step of the way."

"We had better get the grill fired up because we will have dinner guest soon."

"Don't you do a thing. I will take care of everything."

"I am not helpless. I will start preparing the meat and vegetables for grilling." Frank heads out to fire up the grill, and Debbie begins to prepare the food for cooking.

—᠓—

Debbie and Frank are busy preparing the grill and the food for their dinner. Soon the doorbell rings and Debbie rushes to open the door to welcome Pam, Joe, and their kids. Debbie informs Joe that Frank is out back preparing the food and asks Joe if he would like a beer. At the same time, she tells Regina and Joe Jr. that the girls are in their room playing video games. The kids rush off to the girl's room. Joe accepts Debbie's suggestion for a beer, goes to the cooler, and gets a beer, and heads outside to visit with Frank. Debbie continues to get eating utensils and the remainder of the food preparation ready for dinner as she and Pam enter into conversation.

Debbie begins to tell Pam about the problems that their mom suffered from before she passes away and suggested to Pam that with the family history of breast cancer that maybe she should be checked for any signs. Pam looks a little puzzled at this line of conversation from Debbie and asks her sister what brings on this line of discussion. Debbie tells Pam that she went to see her doctor and requested a mammogram and the results were not all positive. Pam asks Debbie if she cares to explain, and Debbie tells Pam that her doctor has found something and wants to run further tests. "There is no confirmation of anything, but due to our family history, she wants to run more tests, and I have and appointment to see her Tuesday. That is my reason for this little get-together tonight. I have already told Daddy. Maybe I should call him and invite him over. That is if he is not busy."

Pam tells Debbie that she will call him. Pam expresses concern with this information from Debbie as she places a phone call to their dad. James answers the phone, and Pam immediately asks him if he is busy. James informed Pam that he has dinner date with Claudette. He asks Pam if there is anything wrong, and Pam informs James that she, Joe and the kids are at Debbie and Frank's. They are preparing dinner. She and Debbie would like to know if he is available for dinner. James asks Pam the time that dinner would be served, and Pam tells him that it has not been prepared yet. James tells Pam that maybe he and Claudette might be able to drop by after they have finished their dinner that they have just ordered. Pam tells James that they would wait for his arrival. James tells Pam that he would have to check with Claudette first to see if it would be okay with her to come over. At which time, Claudette listening to the conversation nods to James that it will be okay with her, and James says, "It is a date." Pam hangs up the phone and informs Debbie that their daddy will come over as soon as he and his date finish dinner. Debbie says, "It is okay for Mrs. Claudette to come over."

Pam is puzzled again and asks Debbie if she understood what she was saying. "I said Mrs. Claudette is with him."

Debbie tells Pam, "It is okay for Daddy to bring her over." Pam asks Debbie to explain her sudden acceptance of their daddy seeing another woman. Debbie tells Pam that she understand now that their daddy is not going to sit around and do nothing. At least she is closed to his age.

"I heard what you have been saying. Maybe it will be good for him." Debbie is not displaying the all outgoing emotional and aggressive personality that everyone is used to. It is very evident that Debbie is worried.

Pam hugs Debbie and says, "Little sis, I love you and will be here for you for whatever your needs are during these challenging times in your life."

—·〜·—

James and Claudette are receiving their food order at the restaurant, and James is not his usual cheerful self. Claudette asks James if there is something going on in his life that she could help him with, and James's response is, "Well, you are going to find out anyway just as soon as we arrive at Debbie and Frank's house. They are all there because Debbie feels that now is a time for her to be surrounded by her family."

Claudette asks, "Is she and Frank having problems?"

James says, "No, it is nothing like that. You see, my former wife Margie suffered from breast cancer. Breast cancer is the cause of her death, and Debbie being the type of woman that wants to know if there are any possibilities of this disease ever affecting her life paid a visit to her doctor ad few days ago to be tested, and to make a long story short, the doctor found some evidence of something being wrong. I think her doctor found something on that mammogram."

Claudette grabs James's hand and tells James that if there is anything positive out of these tests that this is a disease that she is familiar with and maybe she can be of assistance to Debbie. James asks, "Will you? What kind of experience are you referring to?"

Claudette tells James that she had lived through breast cancer with her sister and she had lived through colon cancer with her late husband. James seems a little surprised to hear these new revelations from Claudette and understands the heartaches that Claudette had gone through because he remembers how life was with his late wife Margie.

Claudette explains to James that her sister's cancer was diagnosed in the early stages and she is now a cancer survivor. "My late husband was not so successful." The mention of survivor brought a little smile to James's face as he informs Claudette that the doctor has informed Debbie that she was not sure of breast cancer, but due to breast cancer being a factor in the death of her mom, it is a good idea for her to be tested even though Debbie is only thirty-two years old, so they are hoping that it is only a scare.

Claudette squeezes James's hand and says, "We will need to rely on our faith in God that everything will be all right." James and Claudette finish their dinner. James pays the check and the two of them leaves the restaurant.

Frank is finishing the preparation of dinner for his family and asks Debbie what he should prepare for her dad. Debbie responds, "I don't think they will be eating because Daddy and his friend Claudette are having dinner as we speak. They had already placed their order when Pam spoke with him, and they will be on their way as soon as they finish their dinner. We can eat."

Frank announces to everyone that food is being served. A short time after the family is sitting for dinner, the doorbell rings. Frank answers the door. It is James and Claudette. Claudette has not met Frank or any of James's grandchildren, so James begins introducing Claudette to his family. Frank provides James and Claudette with seats and asks James and Claudette to have seat and stay awhile with a slight chuckle. The kids finish eating and wanders off to play. Everyone else is seated. Debbie announces to the family that if they had not already heard, she will fill them in on her problem. Debbie proceeds to explain that she has paid a visit to her doctor and requested a mammogram due to a diagnosis of breast cancer that her mom had received after it was too late for her and they all know that she lost her battle. "I wanted to know if there is a possibility that maybe I am a candidate for that breast cancer." Debbie continues her conversation and tells everyone that her results were not all positive and her doctor wants to do some further test by doing a breast biopsy to see if it's cancer. "You see, there is a suspicious mass forming, and she wants to perform what I believe she says is a minimally invasive breast biopsy where she will only use a needle and not surgery."

Frank jumps in by saying he may not know what she is talking about tonight but to check with him tomorrow and he will know something then. Claudette explains to Debbie that she has a sister that was diagnosed with breast cancer and that she is very happy to report that her sister is now breast survivor. Debbie explains to everyone that her doctor had indicated to her that if there is cancer, the chances of it having spread to the lymph nodes are very slim in her opinion. Debbie tells everyone that even though her doctor is making these positive statements, she is scared.

James stands and says, "Let's all pray," and James leads the family in a prayer for his daughter. At the conclusion of his prayer, Debbie makes an announcement on the importance of receiving the mammogram and that this is not an all-female problem because her doctor had informed her that men could also develop breast cancer.

Frank and Joe are surprised to hear Debbie's statement that men can also get breast cancer. The conversation continues mostly on their concerns for Debbie and the disease in general, but Frank and Joe continue to show concern about this new revelation that they also have to be concerned. Debbie explains to them that chances of the two of them are a lot less likely, but she wants her sister Pam to not take any chances.

—⁓—

A few days pass, James is in his office and receives a phone call form his daughter Debbie with the results of her biopsy. Debbie asks her dad if he can meet her for lunch and discuss her results. James becomes a bit nervous and wants Debbie to reveal to him the results but does not ask because he is not sure he wants to know the results, so he decides to wait and Debbie tells him to meet her at James's regular and favorite place that he normally has lunch with family, friends, coworkers, and clients. James hangs the phone up and is very nervous with much anticipation but manages his composure anyway. James informs his assistant Mary that if anyone is in need of his services, he will be out to lunch and he is only a phone call away. James arrives at the restaurant, and to his surprise, he finds Debbie, frank, Pam, and Joe already seated. James asks Joe how did he leave the office and did not tell him. Joe tells James that he was not in the office when Pam called. He is instead wrapping up a deposition and is told to get here as quick as he could. James proceeds to sit, and the waiter presents him with a menu, but James explains to the waiter that he is familiar with that menu and already knows what he wants without a menu. He says that he wanted an ice tea right away and focuses his attention to Debbie and asks, "Is there any good news?"

Debbie informs him that she has not revealed the results to anyone aside from Frank and now is the time. Frank says, "Well everyone is waiting, unless you want me to tell."

Debbie says, "No, I will tell them. The prognosis is not all good."

Frank says, "And they are not all bad either."

Debbie says, "Well there is cancer, but the doctor feels that it is diagnosed in the early stages and perhaps I can live a normal life. The doctor explained to Frank and I that breast cancer treatments have come a long way, and I along with my doctor will have to choose the correct treatment. I can also get a second opinion. I want all of you to know that I am very scared and will be relying on all of you for comfort."

Every member of Debbie's family assures her that she could count on them and assures her how strong their love is for her.

Chapter

Debbie and Frank are at Debbie's doctor's office discussing the kinds of treatments for Debbie, and the questions from both Debbie and Frank are plentiful. What is the primary cause of breast cancer, does diet and exercise make a difference, and are there any advantages to one treatment over another, and the questions just keep coming and the doctor's explanations are at a rapid pace also. After a long exhaustive discussion with the doctor, Debbie and Frank end the discussion with the doctor, thank the doctor, and leave the doctor's office with many of their questions answered. They enter their car for the drive home. Debbie tells Frank that she is confused and frightened. "I know the doctor answered all of our questions."

Frank assures Debbie that she is not alone in this fight, and this is a fight that the two of them will win. Frank starts the car up. They begin the drive home. The drive home is lengthy as they take the drive along a very scenic route. There is total quietness as they drive until Debbie begins to talk by asking Frank if he has reached a conclusion as to what he think will be the correct treatment.

Frank says, "Maybe we should not rush into a decision that we might regret and maybe we should seek advice from other medical cancer experts. You know, a second option or someone that has experienced breast cancer. Maybe a family member, your dad must have some knowledge after his personal involvement with your mom and there is Mrs. Claudette.

Debbie agrees with Frank. Debbie says, "Perhaps you won't like me if I lose all of my hair."

Frank puts his arm around her and, as he pulls the car to a stop, tells Debbie that he will always love her no matter what temporary or permanent change that might take place in her appearance. Debbie asks Frank if he would be able to continue to love her if her breast has to be removed.

"My answer was for better or for worst, in sickness and in health, remember? I said yes to all of those questions. I feel stronger today that everything I said, I still mean it." Frank quickly finds a parking space as he pulls the car of the street to park to continue their conversation. Debbie takes Frank's hand and asks Frank to take a walk with her. The two of them exit the car and start to walk along a very scenic walkway along the waterfront holding hands until they find an isolated spot close to the water and decides to sit and enjoy each other's attention. Debbie tells Frank just how lucky she feels to be married to such a wonderful man. Frank in response tells Debbie that he is the lucky one.

James is at home when the doorbell rings, and as he opens the door, Frank and Debbie are there. James asks the two of them what he has done to be blessed with this visit. Debbie tells James that they just want to talk with him for a minute. James invited then in, and the three of them enter the house and take a seat. James is watching the golf channel on television. Everyone is comfortable and seated. Claudette enters the room and greets everyone by telling them that she is preparing a little tea for her and James and ask if she could get something for them. Frank says that he would enjoy a cup of tea also. Debbie says that she is fine and do not want anything. Claudette tells Debbie and Frank that she does not live with James, but the two of them do spend quality time together. James buts in and says that he and Claudette are joining some friends a little later to attend a baseball game.

Debbie says, "Daddy, you don't have to explain anything to me. You are a big boy. I am here to discuss my upcoming treatment, and I am glad that you are here, Ms. Claudette. You can provide insight from a woman's point of view."

Claudette asks Debbie if she has made a final decision. Debbie tells Claudette that her reason for stopping by is that she and Frank would like to talk with the two of them. "Maybe you can provide us with dome insight as we make a tough decision. We are leaning in a direction, but we are not sure."

James asks, "What direction are you leaning?"

Debbie tells them that maybe radiation will solve her problem because even though she will lose hair, it is aggressive and the hair will return. She and Frank have found out that surgery is not always necessary. "The doctor has advised us that many women are not using surgery automatically."

Claudette starts to explain to Debbie that her sister did not choose surgery and everything worked out for her. Debbie asks Claudette to tell her more about the treatment that her sister used. Claudette explains to Debbie that she believes her sister had chosen a combination of treatments that also included radiation. Debbie asks Claudette if maybe she could introduce her to her sister. Claudette tells Debbie that her sister does not live locally and at the same time, assures Debbie that even though her sister does not live locally, she could at least speak with her by phone. Claudette informs Debbie that here are many support groups that she can rely on and just how important family and loved ones are. Frank holds Debbie's hand and tells Debbie that she is not alone in this fight, and James assures Debbie that is a family fight.

"We are all in this together." James tells everyone that he has taken it upon himself to ask a few questions to do a little research himself. James explains to Debbie that he had found out that there are six types of standard treatments being used and there are also some new types of treatments being tested. After all, he had gone through this fight with his late wife Margie. They did not have the benefit of knowledgeable professionals as there is today. "The first thing we as your family will have to do is begin this process by loving you and seeking the best medical advice and care available with the most qualified professionals we can locate."

Debbie says, "Thank you, Daddy!" The family all gathers in a circle and begins a little prayer. Debbie now knows that she will not be facing this challenge alone.

A few days later, James is in his office working and cannot concentrate as his primary concerns are for Debbie. He knows that Debbie is schedules to see an oncologist that will explain treatment options to her, and James hopes Frank is able to take the day off from work to be with Debbie. James knows how important it is for Debbie to feel supported by Frank. Finally, James decides to leave work and take a drive over to the doctor's office to be with Debbie even though she has told him that it would not be necessary for him to be with her. James arrives at the doctor's office and meets Debbie and Frank in the parking lot of the doctor's office as they have just completed there visit with the doctor and is about to depart home. James greets the two of them by saying, "I guess if I have been a minute later, I would have had to travel to your house to see you."

Debbie says, "Oh, Daddy, you didn't have to come over here. We told you that we would be okay." James wants to know what the doctor had to say, and Frank says there was a lot the doctor told them and they have found out that there is much hope, and just as James had stated earlier, there are options and the doctor did a good job of explaining them. The doctor also has done a good job of answering all of their questions.

Debbie cuts into conversation and says, "We had a lot of questions. We had so many we had them written down."

James asks if they had any plans for the remainder of the day. Frank says that he will be returning to work. Debbie says, "I guess you are stuck with me, Daddy. I am going to call Pam, and both of you will be stuck with me."

James asks Debbie what she wants to do, and Debbie tells her dad that she is hungry but she is not interested in going to a restaurant. She wants to go to the beach and walk in the sand, maybe get a hot dog.

James says, "Sound good to me."

Debbie places a call to Pam to request that she meets with them. Pam says, "Pick me up."

James says, "No problem. We can be at your house in about twenty minutes."

"I will be ready!"

James and Debbie travel to Pam and Joe's house to pick Pam up, and afterward, the three of them drive to the beach where Debbie is able to get her hot dog and walks in the sand on the beach. The three of them also spend some time sitting and talking about Debbie's illness and the types of treatments that are available. Pam had many questions for Debbie. Pam asks Debbie if she has arrived at a decision on the treatment.

Debbie tells Pam that the decision is not final, but she does have a better understanding now as to what her challenges are and the different types of treatments available. The conversation continues for a while until Debbie informs Pam and James that the time has come for her and Pam to depart for home to meet with their primary responsibilities, their children, because they will be arriving home from school soon. Debbie thanks James and Pam for being there for her.

Pam says, "We would not have it any other way."

James agrees with Pam saying, "Debbie, we are going to love you through this challenge. I mean this entire family."

Debbie says, "I like that!" The three of them enter the car and depart for home.

Debbie and Frank are again at Debbie's doctor's office for what they hope is their final consultation with Debbie's doctor. Debbie and Frank hope to make a final decision for Debbie's treatment. This is all taking place after this consultation. Prior to this consultation, they previously solicited and received input from their minister, family, and all of their doctors that they could contact for advice in this important decision-making process. Debbie is also preparing herself to schedule her first treatment and is anticipating just what the treatment will be like, wondering what will be involved. There is much false and misleading input from friends and relative who for the most part do not know very much about cancer treatment other than what they have heard other people saying. Debbie remembers her mom going through her treatment, the loss of weight, loss of appetite, the loss of her hair, and very little energy. Debbie is frightened, wondering if she will see he children grow into their teens, attend their senior prom, graduate from high school, attend college, get married, and provide her with grandchildren.

James is worrying about Debbie, and many of his actions reflect him not being his normal self. James find himself spending most of his time not being very productive, can't sleep well, and not eating well. Claudette had been there for James and Debbie. She is trying to be the stronger person in James's life right now. James is at home watching the golf channel, but he is not enjoying it. He keeps thinking about Margie and her battle with this disease, thinking that he does not want to lose his daughter too. Claudette is spending this time with him this weekend day to try and provide as much comfort as possible. James looks over at Claudette who is sitting and reading a magazine and asks her if she is tired, or would she like to go out somewhere, maybe do something.

Claudette says, "Honey, what would you want to do?"

James replies, "I don't know. I thought maybe you are getting tired of just sitting around with me doing nothing."

"I am not tired of sitting around with you. If you don't feel like doing anything, don't worry. I am content. I want to be with you. I need to be right here with you. I know things are not looking good in your eyesight right now. Debbie is going to be all right. Just have faith. Believe me, it will be all right. Debbie is going to be fine. All of the signs point to her making a full recovery."

James smiles and says, "What would I do if it was not for you?" James gets up from his seat, walks over to Claudette, takes her hand, and says, "Let's dance."

Claudette rises from her seat and says, "There is no music.'

James says, "We don't need any music to dance."

Claudette smiles at James and says, "Let's dance." The two of them begin to dance and dance.

Claudette looks at James as they dance and says, "You are a crazy man, asking me to dance without music." James rushes over and turns the television off and turns the music on and tells Claudette, "Let's dance." The two of them begin to dance again.

—∞—

Debbie is finally beginning her treatment. She soon finds out that there is truth to what her doctor has been telling her all along. Debbie is experiencing loss of appetite for food, which soon leads to weight loss and not very much energy. She feels the weakest after treatments. Debbie's energy level is so low that she is now feeling guilty for not being able to take care of her children. Frank has been a real trooper, so helpful. His job has been very understanding by giving Frank as much time as needed to be there for Debbie. Frank is trying very hard not to abuse the generosity of his employer and has continued to try and carry on with much of his job schedule as possible. Debbie is also happy that she has family support. Her dad James spends a lot of time with her. James is not much help because he spends most of his time worrying about Debbie. Pam has been there for her. The everyday happiness being displayed on Debbie's face is due to all of the support and help that she is receiving from her family. She could never have imagined how helpful Claudette has been to her in this time of need, and she continues to be there for Debbie. She makes sure meals are prepared for Debbie's family and takes care of o all the normal daily housework that Debbie's energy level does not allow her to perform. Debbie is very appreciative of Claudette, especially after the way she had treated Claudette when she first met her. She now understands her father's reason for so much happiness whenever he is with Claudette.

James is arriving for his daily visit with Debbie and also to pick up Claudette. Debbie is very weak from her treatment earlier in the day. There is also noticeable weight loss. Frank opens the door for James and speaks to James, explaining that he is in with the kids, helping with their homework and Claudette is in the kitchen cleaning up and putting leftover food away. James greets Claudette with a kiss and returns to speak with Debbie who is curled up on the couch, watching television. She sits up and speaks to her daddy as he gives her a kiss on the cheek. She then asks her dad to come and sit close to her and let his baby girl lean on his shoulder. James sits next to Debbie, puts his arms around her and says, "I guess this is how we will love you back to good health."

Debbie says, "I guess you got that one right, Daddy, and when you are not available, it will be Frank. He is stuck with me. You are stuck with me too, Daddy!" She is smiling. "I have two men in my life that really love me."

James says, "I guess you do. We are not stuck with you. We love you. As a matter of fact, you have this entire family's attention. We all love you very much. We are all here because we all know that if it was any one of us in need, you would be right there."

Debbie smiles and hugs James and says, "You are probably right, Daddy."

The hour is getting late, and James has an early appointment tomorrow, so he tells Debbie and Frank good night. The kids are already in bed. James departs for home, dropping Claudette off at her house because Claudette has explained to James that she is meeting Brad at her house. After dropping Claudette at home, James finally departs for home and thinks about what his daughter is experiencing. James arrived home and notices that there are lights on in his house. James begins to worry why the lights are on in his house, so he decides rather than enter he would call the police. After a few minutes, a police vehicle arrives with two officers. James notifies the officers that he is not sure if he should enter his house because someone is inside and he does not know who it is. The office tells James that he has done the right thing as he calls for back up. Once the officers have support, they wake the neighborhood by asking, "Whoever is inside of the house, come out now with your hands raised."

They waited for a few minutes with no response. Finally a woman walks out with her hands up and identifies herself as Karen Campbell, but suddenly, she appears to have changed her mind, rushes back inside of the house, yelling to the officers that she lives at the residence with her husband, a Mr. James Earl Lackey.

James begins to brief the officer on the history of his relationship with Karen Campbell and that she is recently arrested at his office with two guns, telling his staff that she and he would be married that day. The officers remember hearing about the encounter. James says, "I think she was released on bond. There is a restraining order that she has violated."

James explains to the officer that the restraining order was issues only a few days ago. The officer in charge say, "I guess we have a standoff now that she is back in the house."

James asks the officer, "What are you going to do?"

The officer says, "We will either have to wait her out or rush the house." James does not want to see Karen hurt and is hoping for a successful ending to this situation. The wait continues with communication from Karen telling the officers that they should go away. Her husband will be hone any time now, and they will need sleep once he is there. The communication seems to disappear, all is quiet in the house, and everyone is curious as to what has happened. The decision is made to approach the house carefully and to enter as far as possible. Once inside of the house, it is soon discovered that the house is in disarray, and as they approached to awaken Karen, which he finds to be very difficult. Karen appears to be under the influence of some kind of drugs. They are not able to revive her and calls for the paramedics. Once the paramedics has arrived, they come to the conclusion that she is in serious condition and rushes Karen off to the hospital emergency. James is not given permission to enter his home immediately s it remains a crime scene and is being investigated. James is temporarily homeless until his home is returned to him, and once he has his home back, it will be necessary that it is restored to normal, cleaned, all keys changed, and his security system updated before he will be able to move back in. James is interested in an update on Karen's condition but is advised to stay away from her. James would like to know if her problems could be evaluated because now he is feeling guilty that his involvement with her let to this encounter. It has resulted into what is triggered the problems she is having. Finally after much questioning, James finds out that Karen is very critical suffering from an overdose of mixture of some kind of drugs that is now explained to him. He finds out that she was trying to end her life and is in the intensive care unit at the hospital.

The following day is well underway. James has cancelled all of his appointments for the day, and he still has not had any sleep, shower, or shave and is still wearing yesterday's clothes. Karen remains in a coma, James's family and friend are trying to contact him. James finally checks himself into a hotel. Now that James finally has a place to get some sleep, he has requested that he be allowed into his house which is still a crime scene. He wants to pick up a change of clothes, so he can at least change out of yesterday's clothes. James received an escorted entrance to his house for some clothes and personal items. The officer tells James that his home should be returned to him later today. James realized that he will not be able to move back until he is able to return his house to some form of normalcy. James returned to the hotel and is able to shower, shave, and get a little sleep and begins to return the phone calls that he has been receiving from his daughters, Claudette, and his office to inform them that he is all right. A news crew is attempting to contact James through his office for an interview. James is not interested in any further notoriety on this issue and declines the interview only to find out that other media has located him at the hotel and is seeking an interview. James wishes that all of this would just go away. James places a call to the hospital to find out the condition of Karen and finds out that her condition has been upgraded to serious, from an overdose of pills. James feels a little better even though she remains very ill. The sleep that James did not get is becoming more evident now. James does not want to see anyone right now.

James is finally reunited with Claudette and his family. They are all telling him to check out of this hotel and come and stay with them. James is not interested in moving in with anyone now. He just wants peace and quiet. James tells everyone that he does not want to be a burden to anyone and will remain in this hotel until his house is back to normal and he will be able to move back in. Finally everyone is only calling James to see how he is doing, and they all stop putting any pressure on James to move out of the hotel and give him a change to get some closure on this horrible tragedy that he just had to live through. James feels in need of food and located the hotel restaurant to have a little late lunch now that regular lunch and breakfast has past. Claudette soon joins James for this late lunch. The two of them are seated and trying to order lunch when a reporter recognizes James and wants to ask James some questions about the previous night's events. James refuses to answer any questions. He just wants to place his order for food and maybe get some sleep.

James is finally back in his hotel joined by Claudette. He is trying very hard to finally get some sleep, which has not been easy while thinking about all that has happened in his life during the last twenty-four hours, as well as his concern for Debbie. After a lot of trying and constant interruptions, James is finally asleep. James sleeps continually until late in the middle of the night when he wakes up. Claudette is asleep, and James is unable to return to sleep. He does feel much better after this rest and now feels that he can return to his office to work.

—⚏—

It is early morning. James unable to get anymore sleep is up and ready for breakfast and a trip to his office. Claudette awaken by all of James's activity looks up at James and asks if he is able to get any sleep. James, smiling, says, "I feel like a new man with a fresh shower, shave and dressed to meet the world."

"I must have been a whole lot of fun last night."

"We were both very tired, hungry, and sleepy. We are now rested, and I am ready for a big breakfast and a day at the office, so come on and get ready to join this old man for breakfast."

"I will do so, sir!" James and Claudette arrive at the hotel restaurant for breakfast.

Later and soon after breakfast, James arrived at his office, and the entire staff was there to greet him and ask many questions about his escapade and Karen Campbell's condition. James is happy that this chapter in his life is over. His wishes are that all will work out for this young troubled woman. He can't and won't forget that young woman's life is in disarray. The help that Karen needs is beyond the scope of James's intellect. He understands that whatever the help this young woman needs must be sought out.

Chapter

9

Debbie continues her treatment which has now resulted in a noticeable change in Debbie's appearance. Debbie has lost most of her hair and is very frail looking, but her spirits are high from all of the support and love she have been receiving from her family, friends, and minister. Debbie and her sister Pam are at Debbie and Frank's house in conversation.

Debbie says, "I guess Daddy knew what he was saying when he said he will have to love me back to good health. I guess that is true for all of my family. You guys really do love me and make me feel good with all of the love that all of you have exhibited."

Pam responds, "We need to direct some of our love in Daddy's direction. You know, with all of what happened to him."

Debbie agrees with Pam. "You are so right." Frank has now arrived home and greets Debbie and Pam with a hug and kiss.

Pam hugs Frank back and says to Debbie, "Now that you have the one you love, I had better head for home. It has been a good visit, sis. I will be back soon."

"I want to thank you for spending this time with me, and I will be expecting your return. I get lonely if I am alone." Everyone laughs at Debbie's remarks.

Frank says, "Thanks, sis, for everything!"

"I must go now. It is time to pick up Joe Jr. and Regina from school."

Frank says, "It is almost time for me to pick up Lauren and Christina from school also."

Pam hugs her sister and Frank and tells them bye as she leaves the house. Debbie tells Frank that she is tired and is going to take a nap. Frank asks Debbie if she has heard from her dad and if so, how is he handling everything. Debbie tells Frank, "Dad sounds okay, but you know Dad, he is never going to let us know everything."

Frank says, "Yes, I know. I hope that woman can get some help." Frank helps Debbie up from her seat and into their bedroom so Debbie can prepare for her nap. Frank finishes helping Debbie and immediately goes to the kitchen to prepare snacks for the kids before it is time for him to pick them up. The doorbell rings, and as Frank opens the door, Claudette is standing there.

She says, "I know it is almost time for the kids to come home from school, so I am here to pick them up and prepare their afterschool snack.

Frank says, "Come on in. I was preparing the snacks before I go over and pick them up. You know, Ms. Claudette, you have been so helpful and I am feeling guilty."

Claudette says, "We are just one happy family, and it is my duty to take care of James's little baby girl. You know I am very fond of your daddy-in-law, and maybe you should not tell Debbie that."

Frank says, "She already knows. She might not have been in love with you early in the relationship, but she is now your biggest supporter. She loves you."

Claudette asks, "Where is our little Debbie?"

"She is in bed napping."

"It is time that you go pick up the kids. I will fix their after school snacks. James will be here soon. We have a date." Claudette is laughing. "At my age, I am going on a date. We made plans for this fancy dinner with some company executives that want to retain the James's law firm. For what I do not know, I do know that they want to meet with James over dinner. I hope James is feeling up to it with all he has been through. I don't know why James didn't postpone this meeting with all of the pressure he has been going through and the things going on with him lately."

"I had better be leaving to pick up the little ones, but we will return."

"You get out of here and pick them up. I will have food ready for them when you get back. What would you like?"

"I am okay. Just fix the two of them something." He then leaves. Soon after Frank's departure, James arrived and is greeted by Claudette.

James asks, "How is Debbie?"

Claudette explains to James that Debbie is still asleep. "Franks says that she is tired. She has been enjoying her visit with Pam most of the day."

James says, "I had better not wake her. I will just say hello to Frank and the girls. Are the girls home from school?

"They should be home any minute now."

"At least I will be able to visit the girls." At which time, Frank and the girls arrive home. The girls rush over to greet their grandpa and Mrs. Claudette. James is happy to see the girls and asks Frank if he would tell Debbie that he is sorry that he was not able to wait around, but to send his love and feels that her rest is more important. "Claudette and I have these dinner plans. We will return tomorrow."

"We will tell her. You know Debbie will understand."

James says to Claudette, "The time has come for the two of us depart."

Claudette says, "You just now got here."

James, smiling, says, "And we are just now leaving."

"Well if you say so. I have not had a chance to visit with Debbie either."

James and Claudette say their good nights to Frank and the girls and tell them to say good night to Debbie and how sorry the two of them are that they were not able to visit with her. The girls give both of them a hug as they both leave. Upon leaving, Claudette asks Frank if he can feed the girls the food that she has prepared.

Frank answers, "Don't you worry, we will be all right."

Later in the evening after James and Claudette had left for dinner, Debbie is now awake, saying, "I miss seeing and thanking Mrs. Claudette. I even missed Daddy." The girls are now preparing for bed, but they want to say good night to their mom and have their dad tuck them in bed. The girls hug and kiss their mom and tell her that she missed Grandpa and the hugs are from Grandpa and Mrs. Claudette. They grab their dad's hand and tell their mom good night. Their dad escorts the girls to their bedroom and prepares to tuck them in bed, but to his surprise, the girls request that their dad sit with them a little while because they want to talk.

Lauren says, "Daddy, how sick is Mom? Is she going to die?"

Frank says, "Both of you give me a big hug." The three of them embrace. "I guess I don't have little girls anymore. Both of you are growing into big girls now. Why are you girls asking Daddy these questions about Mom?"

Little Christina says, "My friend Joan that lives next door says that she heard her Mom and Dad say that our Mom is very sick and she might die."

Frank says, "Well it is true Mom is very sick, but she is going to be okay. We will have to love her every day and take care of her."

Lauren says, "Is that why she has not been able to take us to school every day and is losing her hair and always tired?"

Frank says, "We must not depend on Mommy for very much help while, she is sick. We will have to take care of her for a while at least until she gets better."

Lauren says, "We are going to take good care of Mommy. Don't you worry, Daddy. If you are at work, we will take care of Mommy."

The girls hug their daddy, and Christina says, "It is time for us to get some sleep. Daddy, in the meantime, you take good care of Mommy while we are sleep."

Frank hugs and kisses the girls and says, "I don't know what I would do if I didn't have my big girls to help me with Mommy. I will take care of Mommy, and you girls can go to sleep so you can get up early tomorrow morning to help Mommy before you are ready for school." Frank turns the lights out and departs their room to return to be with Debbie.

As Frank enters the room where Debbie is, Debbie says to Frank, "That was a long good night."

Frank says, "Yes, the girls wanted to talk."

Debbie asks, "What they wanted to talk about?"

Frank says, "About you. The girls wanted to talk about their mommy."

Debbie, smiling says, "What did they have to say about me?"

Frank responds with, "They wanted to know how sick you are and if they are going to loose you."

"And what did you tell them?"

"I told them that you are going to be okay and that we are going to have to love you back to good health."

Debbie smiled and says, "Come here and give your sweetie pooh a big hug."

—∞—

The following day, James is in his office conference room with most of his immediate staff for their regular staff meeting. This meeting is almost concluded when the phone rings and James's executive assistant Mary Winfield answers and tells James that Debbie is on the phone and wants to speak with him. James is almost afraid to answer the phone, thinking that maybe something is wrong. James takes the call and says, "Hello there, my little teenie-weenie baby, is there anything wrong?"

Debbie says, "Not much. I missed you last night. I do have some news that I want to share with you."

"Is it good news?"

"I can't tell you. I want you to come over and visit with us tonight. I will explain to you at that time, and bring Mrs. Claudette with you."

James says, "I will see what I can do. What time would you want us to come by?"

"Whatever time is good for you."

James says, "Maybe we can be over around seven. That is if Claudette is available."

Debbie says, "On second thought, Daddy, don't worry about Mrs. Claudette. I already have her with me."

"If you have everything together, the only thing that you want out of me is a warm body."

"Maybe, see you around seven!"

"Seven it is." They hang up the phone. James turns and looks a little puzzled.

May says, "Does this mean that you won't be available for our office happy hour with margaritas?"

James says. "Well the boss has spoken, and I promise you guys that I will be with you next time."

Mary answers James by saying, "We all understand." James returns to his office to complete his work for the day. James decides to leave the office a little early and says goodbye to Mary and tells her that if anyone is in need of his services, she knows how to reach him. He leaves the office a little early so he has time to pick up some dry cleaning. He can place a call from his car to Debbie to find out more about dinner. James places a call to Debbie from his car immediately after he has picked up his dry cleaning and finds out from Debbie that dinner had been prepared. James departs the parking lot of the dry cleaners and is now driving along the freeway with his favorite music playing in the background and wondering what could the news possibly be.

James finally arrives at the house and rings the doorbell. As the door opens, little Lauren and Christina are there along with Frank to greet him. James greets them with a hug and shakes Frank's hand. He continues toward the room where

Claudette and Debbie are sitting on a big couch watching television. James greets both of them with a hug and kiss and asks Debbie how is she feeling. Debbie answers that she has been up sitting for awhile but is beginning to get a little tired but could not rest until her daddy has arrived so she could let him know why it is important for him to join the family for dinner. Christina and Lauren have good news of their own to show their grandfather. This is the day that Lauren has her report card to show her grandpa, and Lauren is not to be outdone because she has her progress report and a picture of her family that she had painted to show her grandpa. James is happy to see his granddaughters' school progress. Debbie says with a big smile, "I hope you are as happy with my surprise as you are with my two little darlings' surprise."

Frank looks at Debbie with a big smile and says, "I am equally happy for all of my little girls. I don't need a surprise to be happy." Debbie invited her dad to sit on the couch between her and Claudette.

James sits and says, "This must be a big surprise."

Debbie says, "I don't know if it is a big surprise, but it is big for Frank and me." She removes a scarf that reveals that her hair is completely gone, "Daddy, I shaved my head."

James looks startled because he is not used to seeing Debbie with no hair. He is just getting used to seeing Debbie with hair loss. Debbie says, "How do you like me now?"

James gives her a hug and says, "My little girl's true beauty is now truly revealed for the first time."

Debbie says with excitement in her voice, "And the doctor thinks I will be okay."

James asks Debbie if her sister has seen her new hairstyle.

Debbie replies, "Who do you think was with me when I had my hair all shaved off? Yes, she knows! I am still tired but happy. Daddy, Frank and Mrs. Claudette have dinner ready, so maybe we should all get ready to eat.

James says, "That is a good idea. Let's all head for the dinner table and eat dinner and have our usual conversation." James heads for dinner table, trying to get use to seeing Debbie without any hair. Everyone begins to have dinner, and soon after, Debbie tells everyone that she is tired and will be heading off to bed immediately after she finishes eating. Debbie has not had much of an appetite for food lately, especially after her treatments, but she wants to join her family for dinner anyway.

Chapter

10

Claudette, Brad, and Diana are in the car late afternoon driving along the streets, discussing James and his family on their way to visit with Claudette's daughter Peggy and her family. They are also expecting Claudette's son Pearce and his family to meet with them there when Brad realizes that there is a need for gas in the car and he would also like to pick up a couple bottles of wine to carry along with them. While continuing, Brad located a full-service gas station with exactly what he needs, gas for the car and a decent selection of wine inside of the facility next door. While shopping for wine, Brad receives a phone call from Joe Mills, notifying him that Joe would like to meet with him on a possible offer of settlement from the insurance company covering the automobile accident that he was seriously injured in awhile back. Being that the time of day is getting late and it is a Saturday, Brad is thinking this is a bit unusual to be receiving a phone call from his attorney. After speaking with Joe for a short time, Brad and Joe agree on a date and time that the two of them can meet, which made Brad a happy person.

Brad returns to shopping for wine and soon decides on the bottles of wine that he will purchase. Brad approaches

Diana and his mom and informs them that there is movement on his injury claim from the insurance company representing the defendant in his injury claim. Claudette and Diana seem happy that maybe it won't be very long before Brad can put this accident behind him and maybe Brad can finally get on with his life. Claudette is especially happy that maybe Brad and Diana can get married and hopefully bless her with some grandchildren. Brad pays for the wine, and the three of them proceed to car to continue their trip to Peggy and Jim's house. They soon arrive at Peggy and Jim's home and park. They gather their wine purchase that they are bringing to the family gathering. Brad rings doorbell. Jim opens door and greets everyone. Little Alex, eight, and Myrna, five, Olsen along with young Pearce Maddox III, eleven, are also at the door to greet Claudette, Brad, and Dianna. Claudette is happy to see her grandchildren, as they all embrace each other upon their entrance in the house where they find Pearce II, his wife Brenda, and Peggy. They all greet each other as they find seats and continue their conversation. Pearce immediately asks Claudette about James.

Pearce says, "We were looking forward to meeting Mr. Lackey." Claudette blushes as he inform Pearce that James has promised his youngest daughter Debbie, who is recovering from breast cancer, that he would spend the afternoon with her today.

Pearce responds, "I understand his not being able to join us this evening with all that has been happening to him lately. I did get a chance to see him on the news and his daughter's situation which I was not aware of. Perhaps the meeting can take place at a later date. Let him know that we will keep him and his family in our prayers. In the meantime, I guess we are ready to eat." Peggy announces to everyone that drinks are being served.

James is at the home of Debbie and Frank visiting, talking with Debbie and Frank. They are discussing their family and Claudette. Pam and Joe are also visiting along with their children. The continuation of the conversation soon becomes more questions directed at James about his relationship with Claudette. None of their questions to James's surprise is about his relationship with Ms. Karen Campbell. The questions are coming at James on right after another. Just how long have James and Claudette been seeing each other, what plans do the two of them have as a senior couple, does Claudette's family accept their possible relationship, and so on. Debbie stated to her dad that after his running around with all of those young women sometimes not even half his age, now it is Mrs. Claudette. James responds to her that it was all a part of his maturing to his true age after the loss of his beloved wife Margie. Pam wants to know if her dad has any long-term plans that would include Claudette. Joe tells the woman that they should go light on their father. Pam responds, "He is our daddy, and we only have his best interest or what is good for him at heart."

Debbie speaks up and asks her dad if he has ever had discussions with Claudette about her life before the two of them met. James quickly responds with, "I know she was married to Mr. Pearce Maddox I, an accountant and a senior partner in Maddox and Hurrard Accountant Firm. Claudette works at the firm off and on up until her husband passed away. Now her oldest son Pearce II has taken up his dad's place in the firm and is in charge. Claudette is a good Christian woman, the mother of two sons and one daughter, has five grandchildren."

Debbie asks her father if he knows the line of work Claudette's daughter Peggy and son Brad is in. James responds with, "Peggy is an educator. She is a high school teacher. I am not sure of the subject. Brad wants to be record producer, songwriter, musician, and truck driver up until his automobile accident. He now tells me that he is back to playing and writing music, not able to drive his truck yet. Brad's favorite woman friend Diana, whom Claudette is very fond of and wants Brad to get married to, is also a musician, singer, songwriter, and waitress. You might say that the two of them have a lot in common. They often perform together."

Debbie asks James if he knew that one of the reasons Brad was so against Mrs. Claudette seeing him is because he did not want her to get involved with any man that is only after her nest egg that his father had prepared for her.

"I can understand that I would probably feel the same way if it was my mom. We have had that conversation along with many more as we have gotten to know each other."

Pam once again asks her father the question, "Do you have any long-range future plans with Mrs. Claudette?"

James with a slight wink says, "You will find that out real soon."

Debbie announces to everyone that she is a bit tired and will have to lie down for a while. "I hope you will understand because this has been a joyous evening for me, having all of my family here just loving this weak body back to good health."

James tells Debbie that it has been ever more gratifying for him. Peggy, Joe, and Frank echo the same words. Peggy tells Joe that she is ready to head for home and they had better start getting the children ready for our trop home. So everyone starts to say good-byes, telling Debbie to get some rest.

Debbie says, "Well you all have made my day. I love all of you."

James says, "Maybe it is time that I head for home also, and let Debbie get some rest."

"Daddy, you know you don't have to leave."

"I know, sweetheart, but I do want you to get some rest."

—⋙—

James is driving home and is making good time as there are no many cars traveling along this quite narrow road. After driving for a period of time, James finds himself following a car that is traveling at a speed less than the speed limit and very erratic. This car is being driven as if though the driver is under the influence of something when all of a sudden the car runs of the road and over a small cliff. James immediately stops his car and hurries over to see if the driver is okay and finds the driver motionless and seems to be in an unconscious state. James is not sure of what he should do, so he places a call to 911 for help. Immediately after placing the call, he then attempts to revive the driver. James notices that the driver has blood on his clothes and is bleeding profusely. He immediately makes an effort to remember his training and experiences during his services while serving with the US Army Airborne Medics in Vietnam. Deep down inside of James, he is wishing for help to arrive. Finally James is now hearing the sound of the siren blasting and getting louder as it gets closer to him. Soon there are paramedics and police officers surrounding him. The police is asking James if he knows what happened, and the paramedics rushes to the aid of the injured driver. After carefully evaluating the condition of the driver, the paramedics are now telling James that whatever he did is keeping the person alive. They are also telling the police and James that the person is suffering from a gunshot wound. The person has been shot and is in serious condition, and if James had not arrived when he did and administered first aid, he would most likely be dead. The paramedic tells James that they will take it from there. They proceed to prepare the person for the trip to the emergency medical facility and is soon able to place the injured person in the emergency vehicle. The police officers continue to speak with James and informs him they would like to speak with him further after they have completed this investigation, about what he had observed. James agrees to speak with the officers but requests that someone let him know the status of the injured person. This officer recognizes James from his most recent incidents with Karen Campbell and says to James, "I guess you are destined for the limelight. You know, once the media hears that you are there, they will also want to speak with you.

James says, "I understand." The officers tells James that he would let him know the person's name and location of where this injured person is being taken for treatment and he will make sure that James is notified of this person's condition.

Claudette and her family are finishing their dinner and sitting at the dinner table continuing their conversation. The kids request to return to their room to play. Brad all of a sudden stand and says, "Can I have everyone's attention? I, Bradley Maddox, want to announce to all of you, my family, that Diana and I are getting married!"

This announcement catches everyone by surprise. Everyone present is very happy to hear the news. This is just what Claudette has been wishing for. Her emotions reflects her happiness. She rushes over to Diana's side and gives her a hug. Peggy says, "It is a happy time for all of us. This calls for a group hug."

Everyone joins Peggy in a family hug. Pearce says, "This calls for a big toast. My little brother is getting married." Pearce raises the toast and congratulates Diana and Brad. The festive mood continues. Claudette congratulates Diana and Brad. She is now referring to Diana as her daughter and tells her that she is now Peggy's sister. Claudette figures this is a good time to share this good news with James and rushes off to the bathroom to place a call to James. There is no answer. She leaves him a message to call her as soon as he gets the message. The festive mood continues, but there is no return call from James. Now that Brad and Diana have revealed to the family that they plan to get married, they are ready to head for home. Claudette says, "Now that you have given us some terrific desert, you want to call it a night and go home?"

Diana jokingly says, "We had planned to turn in early, not meaning to create any unfinished discussions. We will continue this saga at another time and date."

Claudette says, "Well, we will agree to these poor excuses for a good-bye this time." She begins her good-byes with hugs, kisses, and a good-bye to Peggy, Pearce, and all of their families.

Short time after Claudette, Brad and Diana's departure, Pearce's wife Brenda says, "Now that all if the air is out of the balloon and they have all left, maybe it is time that we go home too."

Peggy says, "Well I guess that will leave poor little old me alone with my darling Jim"—she hugs Jim—"and the kids again."

Brenda jokingly says, "That is probably the way you want it. Just you and Jim alone."

Peggy, looking at Jim and smiling, says, "You are not going to do anything naughty to me, are you?"

Jim replies, "You will find out when we are alone."

At this time, Peggy hears a voice from her little one. "Momma, can we have a piece of cake?"

Peggy jokingly says, "I guess you guys know what that means."

Brenda says, "You guys have the type of fun that we are used to."

Pearce escorts the kids to the car and says, "We are leaving, honey!"

Brenda says, "I guess you can see that I had better load up before I am left here with you guys."

Peggy answers, "Just remember we love you guys. We must do this again real soon."

Brenda says, "It was fun, wasn't it?" and rushes off to the car. Peggy waves good-bye.

James is continuing his conversation with the police officer, telling them everything that he knows. The police speaking with James received a phone call from the office that is at the emergency facility informing him the status of the injured person, telling him that the victim is in critical but stable condition and that the hospital will keep them informed. The officer informs James of the results of the phone call. The officer writes the injured persons name and the name of the hospital on a piece of paper, hands it to James, and thanks him. The officer tells James that he or someone from the department will be in touch with him very soon. James heads for his car and realizes that he has a phone message from Claudette. James places a call to Claudette and find out that Claudette is home waiting for his call. Claudette answers the phone with a hello and that she have some fresh news to fill him in on. James tells Claudette that he also have a bit of news himself. Claudette tells James to go first.

James says, "Lady's first."

Claudette insists, "No, you go first."

At which time, James jokingly says, "Well okay, if you insist," and proceeds to fill Claudette in on all that happened to him while driving home.

"I guess you really do have an eventful like filled with excitement. My news is not filled with as much drama, but I do have to fill you in on my family's happy surprise announcement from Brad and Diana. They surprised us tonight by announcing that they are getting married."

James responds, "Not only is this a big happy surprise but it is also what you have been waiting." Claudette sound very happy and confirms to James that she is exited about this announcement. At the same time, Claudette is experiencing pain and discomfort in her joints. She has been hesitant in telling anyone about her problems, hoping that this is only temporary and will soon go away. James recognizes that Claudette must be dealing with something that she is not telling him. After all, this is a happy moment for her, and he can sense that something is also wrong. James asks Claudette if she is telling him everything.

Claudette says, "I am a happy woman tonight."

"And what else?"

"Well to tell you the truth, I did not want to tell anybody because I keep thinking it will go away. You got to promise me that you won't tell anyone."

"What will go away? And I can't promise anything if I don't know what I am promising."

"If you insist, I want you to keep it to yourself until I really find out what is happening. I have been experiencing pain and discomfort in my hips. Really, all of my joints are giving me problems for some time now."

James asks Claudette, "Just how long have you been having these problems?"

Claudette responds with a little chuckle, "It is my age catching up with me."

"Seriously, sweetheart, I think you should see your doctor and have this pain evaluated."

Claudette tells James that she just so happened to have an appointment to see her primary care doctor Monday morning. "Maybe I will take it up with her at that time."

James agrees with Claudette that she should take it up with her doctor. Claudette asks James is there are any further obligations that he has with the accident that he observed earlier. James tells Claudette that the police officer had informed him that someone from the department will be contacting him with more questions. He does not know when, but he hopes it will be soon before he forgets what happened.

"How is the person doing that was in the car?"

"I was told that he is in serious condition." James now tells Claudette that he is a little tired and is about to depart for home. Everything is over with there, and he needs to get some sleep. Claudette tells James that if he is tired, he should get some rest and that she will let him know the results of her doctor's appointment on Monday. James tells Claudette that he is headed for home and will see her tomorrow hopefully at church, after a good night of rest. Claudette lets James know that she will be at church services tomorrow. Claudette says good night to James and say, "Sleep tight!"

It is now Monday morning, and Claudette has arrived at her primary care physician's office, Dr. Melody Zadikov. Claudette and her doctor become involved in an extensive conversation about Claudette's condition with pain in her joints. The doctor wants to know just how long Claudette has been experiencing these pains. Claudette's doctor is suggesting some test for Claudette as she gives Claudette a preliminary diagnosis. The doctor is not sure of her preliminary diagnosis and recommends that Claudette see a rheumatologist. Claudette asks the doctor if she has anyone in particular in mind that she should see. The doctor tells Claudette that she does and that her assistant will make an appointment for her. The doctor recommends that Claudette try and have her condition diagnosed as soon as possible. Dr. Zadikov tells Claudette that her assistant Karen Blake will give Claudette the information and she will also assist her in making the appointment. Claudette thanks the doctor. The doctor tells Claudette that she wants to see her right after she has fulfilled her appointment with the rheumatologist and her condition had been properly diagnosed. Claudette agrees to return. The doctor tells Claudette that she will prescribe a medication for the pain in the meantime and for Claudette to wait right here in the examining room a few minutes while she writes a prescription. She will then have her assistant help with the appointment for the rheumatologist. Dr. Zadikov's assistant Karen Blake soon enters the room with the prescription and asks Claudette to follow her. The two of them can now make the appointment with the rheumatologist. They both proceed to Karen's office where Karen places a phone call to make appointment. Karen and Claudette complete the appointments and tell each other good-bye. Claudette departs the doctor's office and heads for home, but first she must place the promised call to James and her siblings to inform them of the results of her doctor's visit. Claudette decides to call James last because she thinks that her phone call to her siblings will not be as long. She is surprised to find out the level of concern displayed by all three of her children. Claudette found herself sitting in the parking lot for almost an hour before she was able to place a call to James. She has an even more of a lengthy explanation of doctor's suggestion to James. After a while, James tells Claudette that they would wait and finish this conversation later. The two of them should just meet for a nice dinner at a familiar and favorite location to discuss results of doctor's visit. Claudette agrees. Claudette finally heads for home after her extensive phone dialogue with her family and James.

———

Upon Claudette's arrival home, she is surprised to find waiting for her was Brad and Pearce. Close behind her arrival was Peggy, driving up and parking. Claudette departs from her car and asks, "What did I do to deserve this much attention?"

Brad responds, "Now, Mama, you know we are concerned about your health."

Peggy walks up to her mom, hugs her, and asks, "Mama, are you all right?"

Claudette responds, "I am fine, children." The four of them enter the house, with the three asking their mom questions about the doctor's evaluation. Claudette tells them that the doctor suggested that she have a rheumatologist evaluate her problems of the pain in her joints and that is as far as she have gotten. "The doctor has given me this prescription for pain. I am not sure what these pills are."

Pearce tells his mom to be careful with all of these pain medications. Pearce says, "I had better get back to the office. I only wanted to see if you are okay. I will be checking in later. In the meantime, I am out of here."

Claudette assures all of her kids that she is okay. Peggy asks her mom if she needs her to stick around for a while. Brad says, "You don't have to, Peggy. You head home and pick up the two little ones. I will be here."

Claudette says, "Neither of you have to worry about me. Everything will be fine. Anyway, I am having dinner with James."

Brad, smiling, says, "Well I guess I have been replaced."

"You will never be replaced. It is that James has nothing else to do, and both of you have a life. So go on, I will be okay."

Peggy says, "Okay, Mom, I get the message."

Brad seconds, "I guess we both get the message. Come on, sis." They both leave Claudette alone.

—⁓—

Later Claudette and James are having dinner discussing Claudette's visit with her doctor and the doctor's recommendation that she make an appointment with a rheumatologist. James poses a question as to why the doctor wanted her to see this type of doctor. Claudette tells James that it is because of the pain in her joints and the discomfort she has been experiencing. James asks if her doctor believes that she has rheumatoid arthritis. Claudette tells James the reason for the doctor recommending the appointment is because of her suspicion that Claudette has rheumatoid arthritis. In the meantime, her doctor has prescribed a pain medication. James tells Claudette that he has heard and observed some not-so-pleasant results from rheumatoid arthritis. Claudette explains to James that her doctor had explained to her that there is no confirmation of any disease yet, but if it does turn out that she has rheumatoid arthritis, early diagnosis can help prevent further joint damage. Medication, diet, light exercises, and even acupuncture are ways to control this disease. James smiles and says, "Let's hope it is not that serious. I am ready to order." He calls the server over to order their food.

Claudette says, "I have to look at the menu. I have not decided what I want to eat yet. My plans now are to start eating a healthier diet and not eating everything just because it tastes good."

James asks Claudette, "Are you sure that you know what is a proper diet that you should be eating?"

Claudette says, "Not yet. The doctor gave me a list of foods that I should avoid."

"I already know what I want to order. I will be eating light."

"I will also be eating light."

The food server has remained at their table and says, "If you guys are not ready, I can come back."

James says, "Why don't you do that. We will be ready soon."

Chapter

11

After weeks later, James and Debbie are speaking with Debbie's doctor about the status of Debbie's condition. The doctor is telling Debbie and James that everything is looking pretty good. She can confirm that Debbie's cancer was diagnosed early and the treatment is showing a lot of progress. This particular treatment will soon be over with, and very shortly, Debbie will be able to start growing hair again.

Debbie says, "Well, because I am tired of wearing all of these caps and wigs, my husband and children will soon be able to recognize me again. That is if I will be able to grow some hair again."

The doctor says, "I am sure they will be happy with your progress, whether you have hair or not."

James says, "I can confirm that it is the truth that Debbie is loved by this family, hair or no hair."

Debbie says, "With this news, I would say that our visit with you, Doctor, is pretty much over with. I want to thank you for all that you have done for me."

The doctor replies, "You are so welcome. We have to be thankful for all the progress that has been made in recent years to cure this disease. We are hopeful that this disease is soon eradicated completely."

The doctor tells Debbie that an appointment has been scheduled for her next visit, and it is the appointment that she wanted. They all say their good-byes. James and Debbie depart the doctor's office and are now driving out of the parking area when James placed a call as promised to Claudette. He previously promises Claudette that he will make himself available to be with her for her visit to see the rheumatologist. James asks Claudette to give him enough time to drop Debbie off at home. At which time, he will be over to pick her up. Claudette tells James to take his time. It is still early and her appointment does not take place for another three hours.

James says, "I just want to make sure. I will be there soon." The two of them concludes their phone call as he and Debbie exit the parking area and head for Debbie and Frank's home to drop Debbie off. After dropping Debbie off at home, James departs Debbie and Frank's home. He is driving along thinking about the challenges facing him with the diseases that has become a part of the lives of two of the women in his life that he loves very much. He is also thinking about all of his challenges with Karen Campbell. It just doesn't seem to him that life is being very kind to him. Now that he has reached a time in his life when he should be able to enjoy the benefits of all his achievements. It has been a life filled with hard work and trying to always do the right thing. After the loss of James's late wife Margie, the love of his life, James has experienced many days and nights trying to learn how to live without Margie. It is close to the anniversary date of the death of Margie. James finds himself constantly embroiled in turmoil, wondering if he is living the life that is giving the proper respect to Margie. James believes now finally that he is learning to live a life with meaning again. Maybe now he has found love again but just can't feel comfortable with his finding. This new love is filled with complications by his constant wondering if Margie would approve, or is it the right thing to do. James knows that if Claudette's diagnosis is a disease, should he continue this relationship, remembering all of the hardship that he has experienced during Margie's illness, or would he be doing the right thing to discontinue his relationship with Claudette what he enjoys. James feels that he needs help making this decision and decides to place a call for an appointment with his pastor and friend, Pastor Arnold Bledsoe, to help him make this decision. Pastor Bledsoe has known James and Margie for many years as childhood friends to both James and Margie. James comes to a stop and parks along the street to place a call to his pastor and find out that he can see Pastor Bledsoe the following day. James agreed to the appointment and proceeds to Claudette's home to accompany her to see her doctor.

While continuing his drive to Claudette's home, James is listening to a radio news report when it is announced that Karen Campbell has been released from the hospital to the custody of the police and will probably be arranged and charged for her actions but nothing else reported. The reporter announces that Karen has retained an attorney that James recognizes by name. This attorney is being interviewed by the reporter, but he does not give very much information either, stating instead that he was retained just a short time ago and has not had the opportunity to speak with his client. James continues driving, and soon he has completed his trip to Claudette's home.

LOVE IS NOT ALWAYS EASY

—m—

James arrived at Claudette's home, and Claudette seems to be happy to see him. She welcomes him and reminds James that he is a bit early. Claudette tells James that she was listening to the news and that there is a report that the woman that occupied this house is out of the hospital. James tells Claudette that he was listening to the radio news in route to her house. James's phone is ringing. James answers the phone, and it is the prosecutor's office calling James to notify him that Karen Campbell remains in custody even though she has been released from the prison's hospital. James thanks the person he is speaking with and continues his conversation with Claudette.

—m—

Short time later, James and Claudette are prepared to leave for the doctor's office. After a short drive, they arrive at the doctor's office and proceed to the waiting room to check in with the reception area. They are told to take a seat. The doctor will see Claudette very shortly. Shortly thereafter, Claudette's name is called and is told that the doctor will see her now. Claudette requests that James accompany her in to speak with her doctor. Claudette and James enter doctor's office and are greeted by her doctor who informs Claudette that she does not recognize the gentleman with her. Claudette immediately introduces James to her doctor. James and Dr. Zadikov exchange pleasantries. The doctor suggests that everyone takes their seat. Dr. Zadikov opens up the information folder that she has on Claudette. The doctor begins to discuss the diagnosis with Claudette by saying that she is sorry to say that her suspicion of what ails Claudette has been proven correct. Claudette is free to seek a second opinion if she wants. Claudette ignoring the second opinion suggestion immediately asks the doctor if she could explain to her what exactly does this mean and what kind of life she should expect to have going forward. Dr. Zadikov explains to Claudette that it is true that there are no known cures for rheumatoid arthritis but there are treatments that can allow you to live with less pain and discomfort. The doctor presents Claudette with literature to read and prescription for treatment and medication. The doctor explains to Claudette that she will be recommending her treatment be done by a rheumatologist for this disease. Her assistant Karen will be making the first appointment for her with the same doctor that made the diagnosis.

Claudette says, "How soon should I begin seeing this doctor?"

Dr. Zadikov responds, "I want you to start ASAP. In the meantime, the rheumatologist tells me that he will be recommending a treatment that will make it possible for you to be able to control this disease and give you the opportunity to get on with your life. He will also prescribing pain medication to be taken only if you need them. The doctor will explain to you exactly what will be necessary for you to control this disease. You did read the pamphlets that I gave you, I hope.

"Yes, I read all of them, and I have also read everything that I could download from the internet."

"Good, I am sure we can control this disease and let you live as normal of a life as possible, which should be pretty close to normal. In the meantime, you should take the normal over-the-counter pain and joint medications as needed such as Tylenol until you see the rheumatologist again. At which time, you will be directed toward the correct treatment. I want you to call is office and see him immediately if you are experiencing any unusual problems with this disease. There are side effects for most medications, and the medications prescribed to you will be no difference. Read as much about all of your medications as possible. The doctor will give you advice and answer all of your questions about the disease, plus give you pamphlets to read. Karen will help you make your next appointment with the rheumatologist. I want to see you back here in two months, and that way, I can see how everything is going for you. Just remember, we are going to control this disease and allow for you to continue living a life as normal as we can possibly make it."

The doctor says to James, "It was good meeting you, Mr. Lackey. I want you to see to is that she takes good care of herself and not overwork. I want her to get proper rest. The rheumatology doctor will have a list of food that he will want included in Claudette's diet. He will also want her to follow an exercise regiment. Karen will schedule your next appointment with me."

James asks the doctor if here is any set time schedule for Claudette to begin her treatments. The doctor tells James that the rheumatologist that Claudette will soon see will want Claudette to adjust her diet and exercise schedule. The over-the-counter medication should be taken as needed for pain. James and Claudette are told to remain in the doctor's office and wait for Karen to help with the appointments. Dr. Zadikov reminds Claudette to call her if she is having any problems. James and Claudette to say their good-byes to the doctor and waits for Karen.

—m—

The following day, James is in his office and is having a difficult time concentrating on work. All he can think about is that the anniversary of his late wife Margie's death is fast approaching. He can't seem to get the near death of a young woman that he feels he is the primary cause of all the problems she is having out of his mind. This is a woman that he should not have ever been involved with. James has constant concerns for his youngest daughter Debbie and her illness. While surrounded by all of this, he is spending most of his quality time with a woman that he things he is in love with. James realizes that his assistant Mary Winfield is telling him that Claudette is on the phone.

James answers the phone. Claudette recognizes in James's voice that all is not well with James. She asks him if he is all right. She also tells James that he has not been himself for a few days now. James assures Claudette that he is fine. His only concerns are that two of the most important women in his life are saddled down with health problems. James keeps reflecting on all of the difficulties that Margie experienced during her illness. Claudette asks James if he is still there as James is silent. James assures Claudette that he is listening. James tells Claudette that he has an important appointment very shortly and he will call her after his appointment is over. Maybe the two of them can then discuss any problems that the two of them are faced with. Claudette tells James that she is preparing dinner for two. James says. "Good, I will bring the wine."

Claudette jokingly says, "I will call you around five thirty." Claudette is now sure James is not listening to anything she is saying. Something is wrong. She knows James never drinks beer.

Claudette says, "I will see you around five thirty."

"See you at five thirty.

—⁂—

James leaves work early and is now arriving at the church where he is scheduled to meet with Pastor Bledsoe. James enters church and is greeted by Pastor Bledsoe with an invitation from the pastor to come into his office where the two of them can discuss James's problems. After the initial greetings, Pastor Bledsoe and James sit down for a discussion. Pastor Bledsoe asks James to enlighten him on what kind of worries or concerns that are troubling him. James says. "Well, Rev., you know I was married to my late wife Margie for a long time. Our relationship began when we were high school sweethearts. We had known each other even longer than that. I can remember when we were ten years old and I didn't like girls. Margie was telling my mother that she was going to marry me when she is all grown up. I guess you might say she was my first and only girlfriend. When we were all grown up, we got married and had a wonderful family. You see, Margie was there for my high school prom, during the time I served my country in Vietnam with the 101st Airborne. She was there with me when I returned home and entered college and all the way through law school. Margie has always been my life. Now the fifth anniversary of her death is rapidly approaching, and I am deeply involved in a relationship with another woman that is a member of this church's congregation, Mrs. Claudette Maddox. The Pastor nods, signifying that he knows Mrs. Maddox. "A very fine woman, I might add, and prior to my involvement with her, I guess you might say I tried very hard to forget Margie's death and all of the years we were so happy together by involving myself in many sinful relationships with women much younger than me. One of the women you might have heard about through the media that attempted to take her own life. I guess I was angry at Margie for leaving me so soon. I never believed we would ever be separated. It was not easy for our two daughters either, especially Debbie, and now Debbie is ill. The woman that I have become involve with, Mr. Maddox, found out that she suffers from an illness also. I believe I love Claudette, but I am not sure if this is the correct thing for me to do. I am not a young man. I am a father and grandfather to a family that would be the envy of almost any person my age. I love Margie and continues to love Margie. I visited her gravesite regularly and continue to display pictures and reminders of her throughout our home."

Pastor Bledsoe asks James if the love he has for the new woman in his life has been articulated to her and does his daughters know and approve. James explains to the pastor that his entire family has met and approved of his seeing Claudette, but he has not gone so far as to inform any of them his true feelings for Claudette. "I have not even told Claudette how I feel, but I think she knows I have feelings."

James and Pastor Bledsoe continue their discussion, and the pastor explains to James that Margie has moved on to a calling that God has prepared for all if us and his respect and love for her are on display every day. "That is the reason that we are having this session." The pastor tells James that he has lived a life of faith with Margie, and now that Margie is not with them physically, she remains spiritually in his life. Pastor tells James that it is not unfaithful to Margie to love again. James is feeling much better about himself now that his conversation with Pastor Bledsoe is taking place and that is not being unfaithful to Margie by loving Claudette. James thanks the pastor for his help as he prepares to leave. James departs the pastor's office and then enters his car for the drive to Claudette's house. Before the drive home, James called Claudette to let her know that he is on his way to her house. Claudette tells James that Brad and Diana will be with them for dinner. Brad wants to speak with James and say thanks for his help in the decision on selecting an attorney to represent him.

James tells Claudette, "I will be happy to speak with Brad. Now I can congratulate the two of them on their upcoming nuptials. I will see you shortly." James begins his drive to Claudette's house.

—m—

James soon arrives at Claudette's home, where he is greeted by a smiling Brad, asking James to come right in and sit down. Dinner is now being served.

Claudette approaches James with a kiss to greet him and says, "It will be a few more minutes before we are ready. Brad can fix you a drink of some kind."

Diana hugs James as he sits and says, "Nothing to drink until dinner." James tells everyone that he needs to wash up before dinner and at the same time is telling them that today started out as a rough one but now he is feeling a lot better.

James says, "I went by to see Pastor Bledsoe, and he always has a way of settling a person down."

Brad says, "Diana and I want Pastor Bledsoe to perform our wedding. Oh, I didn't tell you that I have asked Diana to marry me, and not only did she accept but her dad accepted too."

James says with a smile on his face, "I heard happier days are in your future, congratulations!"

Diana and Frank at the same time say, "Thank you."

Brad asks James, "Can we talk for a minute?"

James says, "About anything you would like to talk about?"

Brad sits next to James and says, "I want to thank you for referring me to your son-in-law to represent me in my claim from the automobile accident that I was involved in."

"I am glad he could help you. You know, Joe is a very good attorney, and he is married to my daughter."

"I just want to thank you anyway! The settlement made me very happy. One other bit, I have to get of my chest is that I want to thank you for not taking all my past actions personally. I was not very nice to you, but you were a lot more of an adult about it than I, so once again, I want to thank you!"

James places his hand on Brad's shoulder and says, "You know I am at a loss for word. I will say that I am happy that it has all worked out for all of us, especially your mother."

Claudette says, "Dinner is now being served in the mess hall." Everyone laughs as they prepare to have dinner. Brad agrees to say blessing over the food that they are about to eat. As they all consume the food, there is an especially happy look on Claudette's face. There will not be any further tension between Brad and James. The subject of an engagement announcement party for Brad and Diana is not the topic of the evening. Claudette suggests that maybe she could host the announcement. Brad and Diana could invite both families and their close friends. James suggested that in lieu of cooking food for the occasion to use a caterer. Claudette thinks that a caterer is a good idea. It will save a lot of time and work on her part, and now that she has to discontinue much of her hard work and pressure of hard work that she has been use to. The date of the party is agreed upon and party is set. They all continue their eating with Brad telling James about his not only asking Diana to marry him but he put the question to her mom and dad first.

Diana says, "You mean you asked my parents first?" Everyone laughs and continue there meal.

James is sitting in his office reflecting on his visit with Pastor Bledsoe, thinking just how wonderful the meeting has him feeling at this present time. Now he is beginning to think that maybe Claudette is experiencing similar feeling about her late husband. James thinks maybe this is a conversation he and Claudette should have. Maybe a consultation with Pastor Bledsoe could benefit Claudette also, and just maybe the two of them together could benefit from a meeting with Pastor Bledsoe. James places a call to Claudette and asks Claudette if she thinks that it is a good idea for the two of them to speak with Pastor Bledsoe for maybe a little counseling on their relationship.

Claudette says, "You really think we need counseling?"

James answers, "It wouldn't hurt. It just might help."

"Well if you think it will benefit our relationship."

"I will call Pastor Bledsoe and set something up."

"I will make myself available for whatever time you and the pastor agrees to."

"I will call Pastor Bledsoe right now and get back to you."

"Okay, I will be standing by."

James placed a call to Pastor Bledsoe. The two of them reach a decision on date and time for the meeting. James hangs up after speaking with Pastor Bledsoe and immediately places a call to Claudette to let her know the results of his conversation with Pastor Bledsoe.

Later that night, Claudette is home lying in bed reading and falls asleep. Claudette begins to dream. She is happy and excited dreaming about a larger-than-life, big, beautiful wedding for Brad and Diana. Friends and family of both Brad and Diana are all in attendance. The church is filled to capacity. Pastor Bledsoe is standing tall to officiate the wedding. Seated next to Claudette is her late husband Pearce Maddox I. Sitting just behind Claudette and her husband is her daughter Peggy and her family. Next to Peggy and her family is Pearce Maddox II's family. Happiness is in the air. Brad and his wedding party, which includes his older brother and brother-in-law, are standing tall. The music begins to play for Diana's wedding party's entrance. Finally the doors open and there appears Diana looking very beautiful with her father ready to march down the aisle. Claudette suddenly looks next to her, and it is not her late husband but James Earl Lackey instead, and instead of Diana's father walking Diana down the aisle, it is her late husband walking Diana, sitting in place of Diana's mother is Margie Lackey. The telephone is ringing loud. Claudette is awaken by the phone ring, and she struggles to answer the phone. She finds out that James is calling.

James says, "Hello! Did I wake you up?"

Claudette says, "Yes, but that is okay. I was having a dream. You would not believe that I dreamed."

"Was it that good? I hope I was in it if it was good."

"Boy, were you in my dream. I was dreaming that the wedding for Brad and Diana was taking place. I could see you, your wife Margie, and my late husband involved in the wedding. It is a very long story that I will have to fill you in when I am not sleepy."

"Well, if you are sleepy maybe, I should fill you in later."

"I am not that sleepy, tell me, and tell me everything."

James, laughing, says, "I hope whatever my involvement in the wedding was positive."

"You might say it was all positive and confusing."

"I know it is late past your bedtime. I had another long lengthy counseling conversation with Pastor Bledsoe about our relationship."

"I thought I would be involved."

"You will be involved as I explained."

"What about our relationship?"

"I have very strong feeling for you and maybe plans for a more permanent future with you."

"Yes, go on."

"You know I am not with you because I have nothing better to do. I love spending time with you. I also have strong feelings for you."

"I am somewhat confused because I still have strong feelings for my former wife Margie and have been thinking that maybe it is not fair to you. You know, my still having feelings for my wife even though she has passed away."

"I loved my husband. He has passed on, and I feel that he loved me in return just as much. I understand he is gone, and I feel that he would want me to move on with my life. I know I would want that for him. My children are very happy for me now. They really, really did love their father. They loved their father so much that I don't have to tell you about Brad's reaction to my seeing you."

"Yes, I know. That is my reaction for asking you to join me in a counseling session with Pastor Bledsoe."

"I told you that I do not have a problem with that. I will be happy to join you."

And I want to thank you for joining me. Pastor Bledsoe thinks it will be a good idea also. You know, he has a very good opinion of you. Maybe you can tell Pastor Bledsoe and me about that dream I woke you up from when we meet."

Claudette, laughing, says, "Maybe so."

"I love you, until tomorrow. I am going to let you go back to sleep."

Claudette, surprised at James saying "I love you" says in return, "I love you too." She then says good night.

—⅏—

The following day, James calls Claudette to discuss their upcoming meeting with Pastor Bledsoe and the revelation that they both had discussed last night. The meeting with Pastor Bledsoe will include dinner which was little suggestion of his to the pastor. "The meeting will take place at my house with a home-cooked meal prepared by yours truly."

Claudette is laughing. "Home-cooked meal that you are cooking?"

"That is correct. I am cooking."

"Maybe you can pull this off with a little bit of help from take-out."

"It has to be a home-cooked meal. That is what Pastor requested."

"Maybe I will help,"

James, jokingly, says, "I was hoping you would say that, so does that mean that everything is a go?"

"I guess it is a go only if I am rewarded."

"What kind of a reward?"

"I will tell you later."

"I hope it is not too much. After all, you are dealing with a desperate man."

"We will see. You know with all of the health problems I have been having lately, I need this session, and maybe he can calm down some of my fears."

"You can never tell. He just might. I will have to contact Pastor Bledsoe tomorrow and confirm this meeting for this home-cooked meal."

"I want you to know that I will be spending the afternoon with Brad and Diana selecting a menu for their wedding announcement with the caterer that you provided the name for."

"Good luck on that. Out office had used this caterer on several occasions for small affairs. You know less than one hundred people."

Claudette tells James that Brad and Dianna are here.

James says. "I had better let you go." The two of them says their good-byes. Immediately after Claudette hangs the phone up, it rings again. This time, it is the rheumatology doctor's office calling to tell Claudette that the doctor would like to see her as soon as tomorrow if it is possible. Claudette accepts the request and asks the time and the reason for the visit. Claudette is told that the doctor would like to inform her about treatments and medications that she will be prescribing. Claudette hangs up the phone from the doctor's office and notices that Brad and Dianna have let themselves in and are ready for her input. Claudette is instead now worrying about the treatment for the rheumatoid arthritis will involve and that worrying about it will not solve anything, maybe getting back to the problem at hand, assisting Brad and Diana in there selection of a menu.

—⚇—

James remains at his office and is very busy trying to make contact with his daughter with no success. He is continually leaving messages for both of them. Finally he decides to take a walk over to the office of Attorney Joe Mills, his son-in-law's office, to find out if Joe has any idea where is wife and her sisters are at. James's arrival as an unannounced guest to Joe's office results in James finding joe on the phone with Pam.

Joe says, "Be with you in a minute. Dad, I have your daughter on the phone, and she is with Debbie."

James is now thinking, *I have found both of them. Coming over here was not a bad idea.*

Joe all at once hands the phone to James and says, "She wants to speak with you, Dad."

James, taking the phone, says, "Hello?"

Debbie is now on the phone and says, "Daddy, I think I have some good news about my cancer. The doctor says that there are no signs of my cancer spreading. As a matter of fact, it has regressed."

"Oh, my baby, that is the best of the best news!" James sits as he is talking to Debbie.

"Yes, Daddy, that is the best of the best news. I have not told Frank yet."

"I had better get off this phone so you can let your husband in on this joy. I had been trying to call you and Pam all morning and was unable to reach either of you. I am so happy that I was able to speak with you, and I am going now."

"Good-bye, Daddy, I will call you later." James hands the phone to Joe and is very happy with the news as he departs for this office, remembering once he arrived at his office his conversation with Brad and Diana, especially the news about how happy he is with the results of Joe's handling of his legal matters. James immediately calls Joe and asks Joe if he is busy for lunch.

Joe tells James, "I will not be taking lunch on time because I have a lunch schedule with Brad Maddox, a client that was referred to me by you. I think he is the son of your friend, Mrs. Claudette.

James jokingly says, "Yes, I believe I do remember him. You guys enjoy your lunch."

"We can do lunch tomorrow, I am not busy."

"Tomorrow is too late, never mind."

—m—

James is sitting quietly in his office viewing a photograph of Margie that he continues to display in his office when he receives phone call from Claudette telling him that she received a phone call from the rheumatologist office requesting to see her as soon as possible.

James asks, "Did they tell you the reason for wanting to see you?"

Claudette says, "The doctor wants to see me to brief me on the treatments the he is prescribing to control my rheumatoid arthritis."

"That is good. Sounds like your doctor wants to start taking care of business."

"I am a little nervous. I don't know what to expect."

"Well it won't be bad whatever the doctor will be prescribing. You can at least expect positive results of what the doctor will be prescribing that will allow you some relief from pain and discomfort. You will probably sleep better and relax easier."

"You made me feel better already."

James jokingly says, "That is what I am here for."

"Let me get back to what I am doing, I will see you later."
"I hope not too much later!"

James is once again thinking about his late wife Margie and the guilt that he has been advised to not feel. Maybe he would go for a walk around the busy neighborhood. James does decide to go for a walk. As James walks the street, he finds that the streets are very busy and everybody is in a hurry, but at least his mind is much more active in a positive way. He finds himself thinking about many things that makes him feel much happier. James continues to walk and looses track of time. Before he realizes it, he has walked completely out of the neighborhood and has to seek transportation with a cab to get back to the office in time for an appointment. James has found that walking is refreshing today and maybe he should do it more often. James arrived back in his office and finds his appointment with a client is on time. He also finds out that Claudette would like for him to be with her for her doctor's appointment tomorrow. James looks at his calendar for tomorrow and realizes that he is scheduled for a deposition tomorrow on behalf of the clients he is meeting with now. He quickly calls Claudette to let her know that he will not be available tomorrow or the next two days. Claudette tells James that her asking that he be with her tomorrow is wishful thinking anyway and that she understands.

James says, "I promise to make it up to you."

"I will be all right. You take care of your responsibilities, and I will see you when it is all over with."

"Thank, I am off to work."

Claudette is seated at the doctor's office, and the doctor is explaining to Claudette the treatments that he is prescribing to her and when it will all begin. The doctor soon completes his explanation of the treatments. He asks Claudette if she has any questions. Claudette, pulling a couple of sheets of paper with questions written down on them, tells the doctor that he has already answered most of the questions that she has written on her notes and that he only missed a few.

Claudette says, "Doctor, can acupuncture be helpful?"

The doctor explains to Claudette, "Some doctors do prescribe acupuncture, and if you ever consider acupuncture, I can recommend someone to you."

"I will wait on that option. Let me give what you are prescribing a chance first, and second, I am afraid of the idea of all those little needles sticking in me." She smiles.

The doctor assures Claudette, "If you and I manage this disease properly, you should be fine, not pain free but managed pain, and do not even think about early death or twisted joints," Claudette thanks the doctor as she prepares to leave his office.

Few days has passed, James is driving along the waterfront heading for home. All is very scenic, sun shining and beginning to set in the west, comfortable temperature, and people strolling along the beach. James still cannot get over the fact that the continues to love Margie, knowing that Margie will not be in his life again. James just cannot get Margie out of his thinking. James and Claudette have already enjoyed their successful dinner counseling session with Pastor Bledsoe. At least it was a success for Claudette, and she feels that her life with her late husband was filled with lots of love and respect. Claudette's concern these days is to find relief and hopefully some day a cure for rheumatoid arthritis. She has found love again in James Earl Lackey.

James is now looking for and finds a place to part. He exits his car to join all of the other people taking in the beauty of the beach. James soon realizes that he is a man strolling the beach with a shirt and tie. This looks a bit out of place. James takes his shoes and tie off, rolls his sleeve up, and continues along his path on the beach, trying to clear his mind, trying and giving complete thought to Claudette. James finds this very hard to do because his mind keeps returning to Margie. James knows that he enjoys being with Claudette. Now he is beginning to think that he should refrain from seeing Claudette for a while and then he will miss her. Maybe once he does miss her, his true feeling will emerge and overcome any other feelings that he has for Margie. The loneness will help him understand that he only loves Claudette now.

James has not seen Claudette for a few days. The date of Brad and Diana's engagement party has arrived. James tells Claudette that he will not be able to attend due to an emergency meeting in another state. "Please express my regrets for not being there to the future bride and groom. I will be at the wedding. "Claudette is very disappointed that James will not be attending the announcement party but tells James that she understands and will see him once he returns from his trip. James does feel bad about lying to Claudette. James feels that this lie is necessary to find out if there will be any disconnection from Margie and just how strong his love for Claudette is.

—⚬—

James is alone and lonely. He knows that this choice is his. James is off from work. His calendar has been cleared of all appointments due to his being out of town for business the next ten days. Mary has instructions to not tell anyone the reason for James not being in the office, especially to his family and Claudette. James decides that is he really wants to be out of touch, he should take an out-of-town trip to a resort or cruise. A seven-day cruise will allow James time to return home in time for the anniversary of Margie's death. James does not want to miss that day, because his plans are to visit Margie's gravesite on that day.

—⚬—

James begins his cruise, and just before his departure, he decides to call Debbie and Pam to let them know that he is really embarking on some alone time and will be home for the anniversary of the death of their mom. The cruise ship departs. James is trying to relax in his cabin when he realized that he has a balcony to sit and view the ships departure while trying to read some of the reading materials he has with him. James is not able to focus on what he is reading. He begins reflecting on his most recent cruise with Karen Campbell instead, so he decides to take a walk around the ship to see what is available for entertainment for the next seven days. James finds out that this is a very nice cruise ship that provides enough fun and entertainment to keep even a sad person upbeat. James finds himself very lonely for Claudette's companionship and starts to hang around the pool area ordering drinks. Drinking soon becomes his daily routine. The only entertainment for James is drinking wherever there is a drink, and eventually he ends up asleep in his room.

—◊◊◊—

Claudette has not heard from James. Whenever she call James, her calls went straight to voice mail. She calls James's office number but is told that James is out of town on business and would be back in the office in a few days. Claudette is now beginning to think something is wrong or James is trying to purposely avoid her. This is not like James, not calling or being out of touch from her. She thinks maybe Pam or Debbie just might know if anything is wrong with James or if he is trying to avoid her. Claudette calls Debbie and Pam but finds out that neither of them can give her the answer. They could only tell Claudette that their father is out of town and would return in a few days. He is not trying to avoid her. He loves her very much.

—◊◊◊—

Debbie being the aggressive woman that she is takes it upon herself to locate her dad and find out his reason for letting his life become so unraveled. After all, her mom passed away over five years ago, now her father is acting like an immature person. Debbie calls Pam and let Pam know that she intends to locate their father and find out why he is letting his life become so unraveled. Pam advised Debbie to not get involved in their dad's immediate situation now; instead, they should be there to support him, and he does need their love and support.

Debbie says, "He does need out love and support, but I am still going to find him and let him know how I feel about his actions." Debbie says good-bye to Pam and immediately calls the travel agent that normally books her dad's trips. Debbie has found the goings rough as no one is giving out information on her dad. Finally with persistence and verbal threats of having her dad discontinuing doing business with this agency and stretching the truth about her reason for wanting to locate her dad, she is able to get the information that she needed to contact her dad. Debbie immediately placed a call to the ship that her dad is travelling on. She leaves an emergency message for her Dad to call her immediately.

—⚶—

James receives message to call his daughter Debbie immediately. James begins to wonder if something is wrong and starts to try to call Debbie to find out why the urgent call. Debbie answers phone by saying hello before she realizes that it is her dad calling. James asks Debbie is there is anything wrong.

Debbie says, "Yes, Daddy, you have exiled yourself from the rest of us. You don't call or anything. How do you know that we are not in need of you?"

"I am sorry, baby. I just felt that I needed some time away to clear my head or some things."

"We miss you. When are you coming home? Ms. Claudette is thinking that something is either wrong with you or you have love interest other than her."

"It is nothing like that, baby. I will be home in two days. Tell everyone that I love them and miss them, and I will see everyone in two days."

"You did not have to throw this big of a shock in our lives."

"I am truly sorry for my actions. I just miss your mother so much, and I know that she is not coming back. I have done a lot of soul searching. I think now I can do what I believe your mom would want me to do. That is to get on with my life, love you and the rest of my family, and doing what I am doing now only complicated life for all of us."

"Mom would want you to be happy, and if being happy means that you will have a life with Ms. Claudette, who I know loves you very much, then that is what mom would want for you."

"Sometimes my little girl doesn't act like a little girl anymore. She is all grown up now. Maybe Daddy should sit down and listen to her before he rushes off and make these stupid and unwise decisions."

"I will see you in two days."

James is attempting to call Claudette but find it difficult, trying to figure out a good reason for his actions. James knows that his disloyalty to Claudette for his deceased wife is not going to sit well with Claudette who has faced similar hardships with her life. James returns to the bar to have a drink and to reflect on his actions and reflect on whether his actions are excusable. James finds out that drinking is not giving him any answers. He returns to his cabin to think about how he will face Claudette. After a short time, James falls asleep and begins to dream about a life with Claudette, the merging of the two families, and all of the fun with the grandkids. Life seems so complete now, but soon James is awakening with a message to call Claudette. James is now nervous, wondering what he is going to say. Debbie must have told Claudette how to contact him. James starts remembering the old family saying, "Love is not always easy," and that sometimes, "God has plans for us that we might not understand immediately.

Just don't give up. Pray to God and God will relieve you from thoughts that lead you to depression. God is faithful and just, God will answer your prayer."

James is now trying to figure out just what all this means. Maybe his old friend Pastor Bledsoe can shed some light on his reasons for giving thought to what is reciting to himself. James now feels that he has the strength to call Claudette. He does not need an excuse, just the truth. James places a call to Claudette. The phone is answered by Claudette's ten-year-old granddaughter Carey. She wants to know who is calling her grandma. James identifies himself as James Lackey. Carey tells James her name and muffles the phone to tell her grandma that a Mr. James Lackey would like to speak with her. Claudette is happy that James is finally calling her, but she does not want to seem overzealous. She answers the phone by saying, "Hello, stranger, I have a few guests over having dinner with me."

"Anyone I know besides Carey?"

"Yes, you know them all. It is my daughter Peggy and her two children. You met Carey who is ten years old and she has a brother, Franklin, who is eight years old."

"I remember meeting Carey and Franklin. You know, you called me and I am sure I know why you called."

"You do!"

"Yes, I have been away on an unexpected trip, and I don't want to go into details about it right now. I will be home in two days. You have a guest, and you should not be taken away from your guests. I am hoping we can have a full discussion about my trip. I hope you can forgive me. I don't want to hurt you. I just want to be with you. Claudette, the eloquent lady with class, is happy to hear these words that do not go far enough and will wait for James's return."

She then says with a slight tone of anger in her voice, "I will be here." Claudette says bye and hangs up the phone.

James noticed that Claudette is not happy with him right now. He goes to the bar to have a drink but decides against drinking and have a nice dinner instead.

James is finally arriving back home and decides to make his first stop at his office to catch up on work. James calls Pam and Debbie to let them know that he is home. His call to Claudette is a little frigid. Claudette does not have the time to meet with him just yet and does not say when she would be willing to see him. Claudette begins to not answer any of James's phone calls. All of his phone calls are going straight to voice mail. Claudette believes that James has been away on a romantic cruise with some other love interest. Claudette is angry with James. James find himself working late at the office these days, trying to do a little catching up on work that he missed while away. James is on his way home and decides to stop off at the church to see if the pastor is still around. Just as James is arriving, he notices that Pastor Bledsoe is leaving. James greets the pastor and asks if he is leaving. The pastor tells James that he promised his wife that he would be home early tonight.

James, smiling, says, "Pastor, I need you. Maybe she won't mind your being a little late. She is probably use to it by now."

"Maybe she will understand. Come on into my office." James and the pastor return to the pastor's office where James begins to tell the pastor about his trip, his not taking the pastor's advice, and Claudette not answering any of his phone calls. The pastor tells James that he has heard all about his trip and that he really did hurt Claudette, a fine Christian woman with a lot of class.

James says, "I know now. I just want one more chance. I was not with another woman. I have been loyal except for my dealing with the loss of my late wife Margie, and I hope she will understand."

"Let me let you in on a little secret. Claudette was into my office this afternoon with questions that I told her that only you can answer. I am suggesting that you purchase two dozen roses, call Claudette, get down on our knees and pray to God for forgiveness, and when you are finished, ask Claudette to forgive you."

James tells the pastor that he will adhere to his advice this time. He hopes Claudette will take his phone call. The pastor says, "I think she just might take your phone call this time."

James thanks the pastor for taking his time and asks the pastor to thank his wife for being so understanding.

—☩—

James drives home and heads straight for his computer to order two dozen roses for Claudette. The order is complete, now James is hungry, and his phone is ringing. James answers the phone, and it is Pam.

"Hello, Daddy, how are you doing?"

"I am fine, just a little hungry."

"Do you have any plans for dinner?"

"No, I guess I will be eating at you know where, I mean out."

"We have not had dinner yet and would love to have you over for dinner. The kids want to see you anyway. I guess we all would love to see you."

"You just bought yourself a dinner date. I will be leaving immediately."

"We will be waiting!"

"I will see you guys real soon."

—◊—

Claudette is home the following day with Brad and Diana preparing for Brad and Diana's wedding. The doorbell rings, and Diana opens the Door. To her surprise, there is a big bundle of beautiful roses. The delivery person says, "I have a delivery for a Mrs. Claudette Maddox."

"Diana says, "Mama, you have roses, lots of them." Claudette makes her way to the door to receive her roses.

The delivery person says, "Sign right here, ma'am."

Diana says, "I will sign."

Brad rushes over to see the flowers. "Somebody loves my mama besides me."

Claudette says, "Shut up, Brad," as she takes her flowers and reads the enclosed card with the biblical quotation, "Be kind and compassionate to one another, forgiving each other, just as Christ God forgave you." The card also reads, "Sometimes it is hard, but please forgive me, and maybe then we can start the healing process. God will give you all of the help you will need. I will be here waiting to embrace your response to my apology." Claudette is overcome with emotions after reading the card. Brad and Diana want to read the card. The two of them read the card but do not understand the reason for the card. Claudette tells them that only her needs to understand what the card is saying.

Brad says, "That Mr. Lackey must have made Mom angry, and now he wants to apologize."

Diana responds, "You should just leave it alone."

"My bad!"

Claudette feels that she owes James a phone call.

—∞—

James is at work, still catching up with the work that he missed. He is very busy when he receives phone call on his cell phone, and it is Claudette. James says, "Hello, James Lackey here."

Claudette answers jokingly, "My arthritis can't take a lot of stress."

"I was hoping you would call. How is your arthritis?"

"It feels a lot better now that I have all of these beautiful roses to soothe the pain of this sixty-something-year-old woman."

"This sixty-something-year-old man is dying to look across a quite beautifully decorated table at an eloquent restaurant in a quite corner having a nice meal with this sixty-something-year-old woman."

"I will have to think about that invitation. If the sixty-something-year-old man is worthy. Okay, I thought about it. I accept."

"Pick you up at six thirty."

"I will be ready!" James quickly gets up from his desk, a little overcome with excitement.

—∞—

Later that evening, Claudette and James are seated in the restaurant. They both seem very happy and even though Claudette feels that there still remain unanswered questions as to James's unexplained disappearance. Claudette is telling

James how much his disappearance hurt the once that love him most, his family.

James says, "I hope there is forgiveness in my future."

Claudette replies, "Sometimes it really is difficult to forgive. I am a woman of faith that believes that if there is forgiveness in this world, I want to be part of it. You know my door will always be open to you, James. I forgive you and hope you are forgiven by Pam and Debbie. The two of them and their families missed you. I had a conversation with Pastor Bledsoe. He made it clear to me that I can forgive."

"I am so thankful for the understanding of my wrongdoings. I took a cruise to get away from problems that I do not have. I am surrounded by love."

"I am thankful that you are finally understanding just how much you are appreciated and loved."

"Believe me, I do!" Claudette now tells James that maybe it is time for them to order their food and enjoy the evening just as she observed the server arriving to take their order. James is not ready to order and tells the server to give them a minute.

The server says, "Take your time, sir. Just let me know when you are ready."

The next day, James is kneeling next to Margie's grave speaking in a soft voice tone, telling Margie that he heard her message and wants to thank her for making it clear to him in her message that he should move on with his life. James is saying that their family is well. "Debbie has experienced a little setback with a problem that you are very familiar with. Debbie's illness is coming along just fine. All reports from the doctor are that she will be fine. The grandchildren are growing up. You would be so proud of them. We have two that want to follow in Grandpa's career path and become lawyers. Joe Jr. is now eleven and wants to be like his daddy and grandpa. He wants to become a lawyer. He also wants to become a professional football quarterback or major league baseball pitcher. Regina is nine and Christina who is six have not made up their mind yet about a career. I think Regina has her eyesight on becoming president of the United States. All four of them play sports. It is just Joe Jr. takes this athletic skills much more serious. I feel much more vindicated for the direction that my life is headed, knowing that I no longer feel any quilt for my new relationship with Claudette or any anger over your early death. Rest well, my dear. I still love you."

It is now Saturday morning. James is home alone sitting at the breakfast table finishing up his breakfast and reading the morning newspaper. The doorbell rings. James thinking that is a solicitor takes his time answering the door. James opens the door, and to his surprise, standing there is his older brother, Samuel Earl Lackey, with a big smile on his face. James is pleasantly surprised to see his brother. Sam does not visit very often. He would rather entertain than be entertained. Sam has such a large family. He and his wife Carol have seven children of their own and seventeen grandchildren. James and Sam are happy to see each other. James invited Sam o come on in, sit down, and have a little breakfast. Sam tells James that he has already had breakfast, but he will have a cup of coffee. James pours Sam a cup of coffee and points to the cream and sugar. Sam says, "You know I like my coffee strong with nothing on it."

James says, "Yep, I do seem to remember that. How is the family and what brings you this day? I thought you normally work on Saturdays."

"Normally I do, but you know I don't have to spend every moment there these days. I now have sons and daughters that are all grown up, educated, and even have a couple that wants to grow my business by taking over while I retire and get out of their way. So here I am over here with my little brother."

"Are you ready for retirement?"

"Carol and I have saved up a little nest egg. We are going to shop for one of those long recreational vehicles and hit the road. You know, see the USA. By the way, how is your golf game these days?"

"I play occasionally. If you want to play, I can get us a tee time. I have played with your crew recently and that Patty always wins."

"She handles me too, but let's go out, if you can find a couple of duffers that we can beat."

"I just know that right two. I will place a couple of calls, get dressed, and off we will go."

James and Sam are leaving to play golf. Sam is reminding James of the old days when he and James were young preteen-agers.

Sam says, "James, you remember our young days as boys growing up, and Daddy loved taking you and I to ball games, whatever ball game was taking place, baseball, football, basketball. No matter the ball game just as long as it was a ball game, we were there. We would take Mom and Mary shopping, drop the two of them off, and tell them that we would be waiting in the car. We would be waiting in the car all right, heading for the old ball game. They would never miss us. When we returned, they would be still shopping. You remember Mom was cheap, never buying anything but still shopping anyway without making a purchase. Daddy would say, 'Honey, are you tired yet? We are!' Mom would say, 'It is getting late. Let me pay for these stockings so we can go home. My boys must be tired. Mary and I have been having a good time shopping.'"

"Yes, Mom always bought stockings. She must have had enough stockings to last two lifetimes. Why don't we do something different today? Let's go to a ball game for old times' sake and to remember Mom and Dad."

"I must make a call myself so I won't be expected too soon either."

James and Sam place their phone calls and prepare to leave for the golf course. Sam asks James about Claudette. "Is this your new girlfriend? Has my little brother gone and got himself a girlfriend? I do remember Pam and Debbie being upset about you dating all those young girls younger than either of them."

James is smiling and says, "I will tell you all about Claudette and all of my recent experiences. We have whole day and part of the night to talk." The two brothers leave laughing.

—⚭—

It is now Monday morning. James is in his office with a little free time after finally catching up on his work. There is a lot of happiness showing on his face. He feels that he has patched up things with Claudette, Debbie is on the mend, spent a good day with his older brother, and James could not be happier. Things are going great. Attending that Saturday baseball game really has brought back some pleasant memories, thinking about the wonderful relationship two brothers and their sister enjoyed growing up in a home filled with so much love. Two of the most wonderful parents that anyone could ever wish for. Pam and Debbie's acceptance of Claudette is now growing very positive, and Claudette's family accepts him. James's executive assistant Mary Winfield rings James and tells him that his sister-in-law is on the line.

James answers the phone, "James Lackey here."

On the other end is Carol Lackey crying. "I don't think he is going to make it."

"Who isn't going to make it?"

Carol says, "Sam. The paramedics just arrived at the hospital with Sam and I, and they told me that he is in bad shape."

"What hospital?"

"You know the one over by our house." She attempts to ask someone the name of the hospital and the location. She is unable to remember the hospital's name or location withal of the confusion taking place.

James says, "Don't worry, I know. I am on my way."

James tells Mary to cancel his appointments for the day. "I will be in touch. My brother is in the hospital. I don't know what is wrong. I am on my way to the hospital, will be in touch with more information when I get more." James leaves in a hurry. As he is exiting the building parking lot, he is closed to having an accident. The driver that he nearly has an accident with flips him the bird as he exits the parking lot. James does not respond, just slow down, and exits the parking lot to head for the hospital.

—∞—

James is now entering the emergency area of the hospital where Sam is being attended to. He observed Sam's daughter

Melissa. James rushes up to Melissa who is crying saying, "Oh no! Not daddy. Uncle James, Daddy is not going to make it. We are losing him."

James embraced his niece and says, "Where is he? What room is he in?"

Melissa tells James, "Only two people at a time can be in with Daddy. Mom and Aunt Mary are in with him, right now." James and Melissa have a seat as all of Melissa's sisters and brothers are now arriving. James begins asking if there is a doctor that he can speak with. James is told that the emergency room doctor on duty will speak with the family ASAP. James's sister Mary finally is out for James to speak with. She tells the family that Sam had a massive stroke. He is alive but in very critical condition.

"I do not have any good news to report. It is touch and go." James pulls the family in a circle to all pray. The emergency room doctor on duty approaches the family and says, "We are doing all we can. Sam had a massive stroke and will be admitted to intensive care in extremely critical condition." All of Sam's children want to see their father but are asked if they could wait until he is relocated to a room in the intensive care unit. They all agree to do so. Each of them feels that their Uncle James should be the next visitor to their dad's room that is after he is moved.

The day passed into the late afternoon. Everyone has accepted the reality of Sam's stroke. All of the members of Sam's immediate family and many friends of the family have arrived at the hospital. The family's faces are filled with sadness. The doctor enters the waiting room where the family has assembled. He introduces himself as Dr. Shelby Greene. He begins to tell the family that Sam's condition remains the same, very critical. It has become necessary to place Sam on a breathing apparatus to assist his breathing. Sam is not able to breathe without assistance. Carol becomes very emotional and starts to scream out loud. "This means that Sam is not going to make it. Pretty soon you will be requesting to remove Sam from this breathing apparatus. Sam is dead." The family members attempted to try and console Carol. She continues to be very emotional and screaming, "Sam, don't leave me. I need you."

The doctor announces, "We are doing everything that we can." He then excuses himself. James now realized that he had not informed his office of the condition of his bother and it is now after hours. Pam says, "Don't worry, Daddy. I called your office for Joe and briefed Mary on the condition of Uncle Sam. I told her everything." Now entering the waiting area is Claudette and Brad. They are greeted by all of the family. Neither Claudette nor Brad has every met most of the family. She and Brad are introduced to them by James. Claudette knows some members of the family, but Brad knows only James and Joe. He has been introduced to Pam and Debbie in the pass but doesn't remember very much. Carol settles down finally. She is now telling everyone how appreciative she is with all of the support that she and Sam's family is receiving.

"Please excuse my emotions. I am sorry." Carol tells everyone the she is not going home. "My place is right here with Sam. It has been a long day. I understand everyone is getting tired. I suggest that you all go home and get some rest, because there is nothing that any of us can do." No one accepts Carol's suggestion and stays.

It is now late in the evening, and after a long day, most of the friends and family have departed. James, his sister Mary, two of Sam's four sons, Patrick and Gene Lackey, along with Claudette, are now left with Carol. The family members that are left are taking turns sitting with Sam. There is no sign of movement in Sam's body. As the night hour grows late. Patrick and Gene are now leaving with plans of returning tomorrow. James speaks with Claudette about her getting some rest and maybe she should call it a night. After all, her illness demands proper rest. James knows that if Claudette leaves for home, it will be his responsibility to drive her, because Brad left earlier. James decides that it will be best that he takes Claudette home. Mary tells James that she will be there with Carol and if he is needed, she will call him.

James says, "I am going to take Claudette home. She needs rest due to her medical condition. I will be back tomorrow morning."

Two days pass, James remains at the hospital with Carol and Mary. They are very tired and sleepy. Sam's condition has not changed, and they have been told that it is not going to change.

The only thing keeping Sam breathing is the breathing apparatus. Dr. Greene enters the waiting area once again to give the family his latest update. This time, he asks if he could speak with all of the family. Carol feels that she knows what the doctor is about to tell her. She tells the doctor, "I have Sam's sister and brother here now, but I would like to contact my kids and our pastor to take part in this conversation." The doctor agrees. Carol calls all seven of their children and ask them to come to the hospital. She also contacts their pastor to be with them. Soon, the entire family has arrived and gathers in the room for the doctor's report.

Dr. Greene tells the family, "I must be upfront with you. I am very sorry for the news that I am delivering to you. There is nothing more that we can do for Sam. We have retained some of the most brilliant minds in the community, and each one of them arrived at the same conclusion. There is nothing more we can do."

Carol tells the doctor to give them a few minutes. Dr. Greene says, "Take your time. I will be here when you need me." The family gathers in the waiting room. Sam and Carol's pastor Earnest Andrews, addresses the family by reading the Bible verse from Corinthians 15:12-13, "But if it is preached that Christ has raised from the dead, how can some of you say that there is no resurrection of the dead? If there is no resurrection of the dead, then not even Christ has been raised. Christ defeated death, God gives you life and this view is to remind you that the ultimate reward is heaven with God and eternal life."

"Sam is our loved one whom God has prepared a final resting place, and Sam is now about to enjoy his reward as promised from God." The family is controlling their emotions. A short time later, Dr. Greene receives official permission from Carol to remove Sam from the breathing apparatus. Carol asks the family to leave her with Sam. The family respects Carol's request. A short time later, Carol is heard calling for Dr. Greene. The doctor arrived and soon confirms the date and time of Sam's passing.

Now arrangements have to be made for Sam's body to be moved, and preparations will have to be made for Sam's final service. The funeral arrangements are not going to be easy but it is understood that it has to be done. The family makes the arrangements for Sam's body to be taken to the mortuary, and they all soon depart for home. Their emotions are controlled as each member of the family heads for the home of Sam and Carol to discuss final arrangements. Once the news of Sam's death reaches the neighbors, the phone is constantly ringing. People are visiting, bringing food and drinks to a very sad home Carol and her family are very appreciative of all the condolences that they are receiving.

—⁂—

The following day, funeral arrangements have been completed, and the services are set to take place at the home church of Sam and Carol, with Pastor Andrews officiating the services. Per the request of Carol, Pastor Bledsoe, childhood friend to both James and Sam, will attend and give the eulogy for Sam. The day of the services, the church is packed. This is evidence that many people loved Sam. Pastor Andrews is officiating the services, and Pastor Bledsoe delivers the eulogy. The celebration of Sam's life is joyous just the way Sam would have wanted it.

—⁂—

Later that day, after the conclusion of all the services and most of the family and friends have departed for home except for Sam's immediate family, they all gathered themselves at a couple of tables as a family while the clean-up crew is cleaning up. The small grandchildren are playing in the background. Many people have attended these services, and the repass services are where a lot of food and drinks are being consumed.

This makes the family happy. The family is discussing there feelings. James is telling everyone about the wonderful last day that Sam and he spent together. Sam had surprised him with a visit that led to an entire day together. Mary is telling about the last day Sam spent with her. He had also surprised her with a visit, and they had a wonderful day together.

James says, "I believe Sam knew that his time here with us was coming to an end. Sam knew something."

Carol says, "We all remember how orderly Sam was and how particular he was for details. Sam was just getting everything in order for this journey." There is much sadness in the air right now with this family, and at the same time, there is a bit of joy that it is all over. It will be hard getting used to life without that big happy smile that Sam would put on display daily.

Time passed, James is hard at work trying to get over the sudden loss of his brother. He realizes that his mourning period for Sam should have ran its course by now, but it has been very hard on James. His sister-in-law Carol and his sister Mary are not doing any better. Life has not been the same for the three of them. James feels that the more he keeps himself busy, the less time he has to think about the loss of his brother or rekindle the loss of his wife Margie just a little over five years ago. James does have some bright spots going on in his life. His daughter Debbie's cancer seems to be in remission, and Claudette's treatment for rheumatoid arthritis seems to be going very well. Now if he can only get over the loss of his brother, suddenly there is a knock at the door of his office. James looks up, and there standing in the door is his son-in-law Joe saying, "Hi, Dad, are you feeling oly?"

James says, "Yes, I am fine, Just trying to get some work done. I lost a lot of time lately, and I am having a hard time catching up."

"Isn't it about time you take a lunch break? Can I buy you lunch?"

James looks at his watch and says, "Well, you know, I didn't realize what time it is. How time flies. Maybe I should take a little time to eat." James attempts to let Mary know that he is going to lunch but finds out that Mary is already out to lunch. Her lunch replacement is at Mary's desk.

Joe tells James, "Let me get my jacket and I will be ready. I will meet you in the parking lot."

James says, "Will do." He then puts his work away and reaches for his jacket.

—m—

James gives Mary's replacement some instructions and asks her if she would fill Mary in on where he will be taking lunch at. The phone is ringing. She answers the phone and tells James that he has a phone call.

James asks, "Who is it?"

She says, "They say they are from the prosecutor's office."

"I will take it. Let Joe know that I will be joining him as planned tight after I take this phone call." James returns to his office and finds out that this is a phone call from the office of the prosecutor wanting to know if James could meet with them for a few more questions about the accident that James observed. James and the prosecutor agree on a date and time, and they would meet at James's office. James looks up and realizes that Joe has returned and is waiting and ready to go. The two of them leave for lunch.

—ⲱ—

James and Joe arrive at the restaurant, and to James's surprise, sitting at a long table that has been set up for a large group is Pastor Bledsoe, Pam, Debbie, Frank, Carol, Mary, Hope, Kelly, Patty, Patrick, Eugene, Melissa, Grant, and Claudette, waiting for James and Joe to arrive. James is happy to see every one of them waiting to have lunch with him but could not figure the reason. Each of them greets James and Joe as they approach the table to have a seat. The server presents James and Joe with a menu as they are seated. Pastor Bledsoe announces to James and Joe, "I will tell you guys what I have already explained to Mary and Carol, and that is I received a phone call from Debbie explaining to me that this lunch was being set as a surprise for the three of you"—pointing to James, Carol and Mary—"and as your pastor and lifelong friend to this family I figured that I should make arrangements to be here."

Pam says, "We figured you guys needed a little cheering up."

"The check is all your, James." Everyone is laughing. Pastor Bledsoe adds, "Seriously, I want to aim what I am about to say to the three of you, Carol, Mary, and James. It seems that the three of you have burdened yourselves with a lot of heartache lately and give the people who love you most the impression that you want to give up."

Carol says, "Well it is hard after being with a person that you have shared your life with for so long and now you no longer have that person to chare your life with. Sam and I were planning our retirement. Sam often talked about buying one of those extra long RVs and hitting the road. Destination everywhere it would take us. Now I will have to make other plans. It is hard."

Pastor Bledsoe begins to read a Biblical verse from Isaiah 40:30-32, "Even youths grow tires and weary and young men stumble and fall; but those who hope in the Lord will renew their strength. They will soar on wings like eagles; they will run and not grow weary, they will walk and not be faint."

"If you are down and weary or fainthearted, if you are distraught and feels that your loss is unbearable, just let God lift you up. Renew your resistance to overcome as you rest in God's embrace. Let us trust in the Lord because the death of a loved one is sad, but just be encouraged that your loved one is right now being embraced in heaven by God Almighty and your loved one is loving every minute of it. Now that he is in a better place that he had prepared himself for. The rewards are now his to be peaceful with. Let's rejoice now that he is resting and peaceful."

Everyone is paying close attention to every word that Pastor Bledsoe is speaking. The server returns to ask if the table is ready to order.

The pastor says, "Could you come back in a few minutes. Some of us have not decided yet."

Server nods yes. Everyone begins to read his or her menu. Another server is now at the table delivering bread and asking if anyone would like something to drink.

James asks the server, "Could we have a couple more minutes to read the menu."

The server says, "Just let me know. I will be back for your drink orders." A bit of time passes while all is deciding their order. "The chatter is what is good, and have you ever tried on the menu?

The server returns to take orders. Everyone begins to order their food, and once everyone has completed their order, the conversation continues with Pastor Bledsoe answering questions and listening to reasons for their actions by the entire family. Carol cannot hold her emotions in control after hearing some of the questions and answers. She rushes away from the table with Melissa and Patty following her.

Patty says, "Excuse us." It is now very quiet at the table. No one is saying very much. Soon Carol, Melissa, and Patty return to the table.

Carol says, "I hope all of your will excuse me. It has been hard. I am doing much better now."

James is behalf of the entire table guest tells Carol, "We all understand so do not worry about any of us." Mary shows a little emotion also but remains seated as Pam comforts her. The drink orders have been delivered, and now the food orders are beginning to arrive. Everyone is now beginning to eat their food and is enjoying what they have ordered. The mood at the table is very subdued until to everybody's surprise, Carol starts laughing, laughing aloud. Everyone else starts to laugh but does not know why they are laughing. Carol finally starts telling a short story about the first time she and Sam became parents, how Sam was. Carol starts the story, laughing so hard that she is not able to fully tell her story. Now everyone else at the table is also laughing at Carol and her inability to finish her story. Finally calmness prevails at the table. It seems that all of the laughter has changed the mood at the table. Now it seems as if what had been a solemn occasion is a joyous celebration. Everyone is all of a sudden trying to think of funny antidotes to tell. The party last a lot longer than anyone planned. Family members are now rushing to leave the restaurant to get back to their daily obligations and agreeing that the lunch idea is a good one. James asks the server for the check. They compliment Debbie and Pam for the idea of the lunch. Pam rises from her set and says, "Thanks but the credit goes to my baby sister here." She is pointing to Debbie.

There is joyous laughter, as Debbie stands to make her speech and is interrupter by Frank as he says jokingly, "Honey, we must be going."

Debbie says, "You are jealous." Everyone gets up and leaves Debbie for a moment but returns. "For all your rudeness, I am going home to my children. At least they love me." Everyone is now departing the restaurant in a joyous mood.

—m—

All of the gang arrived at the valet to pick up their automobiles and continues with their conversation and tease of Debbie and the success of the luncheon. Joe approaches his wife Pam with a smile on his face, saying, "I don't know how you guys did it, but all of you really made a difference with the family today with all of the smiles I observed on the faces of your Dad and your two aunts. The three of them were pleasantly surprised."

Debbie leans in and says with a smile on her face, "You could not have not done it without me."

Aunt Mary says, "What are you three so happy about?"

Pam answers, "We are talking about all of you guys." She gets a bit serious and points to all of the family as their cars are beginning to arrive with the valet.

James is going around shaking hands and giving hugs to everyone and tells Claudette with a big kiss that he will speak with her later that day and immediately says a good-bye. He then gives thanks to everyone for the pleasant surprise. The valet service continues with the cars one by one, and now it is James and Joe's car arriving. The deliveries continues until everyone has their car.

—⚏—

Back at the office after the luncheon, James enjoyed the fact that much attention is being directed at him. He understands that the love for him by his family is what is motivating everyone's concern. James is also happy for all of the love directed at Carol and Mary. James is now a bit busy. He is up moving around the office and on the phone until he remembers that he has planned to have his car washed and detailed, so he rushes down to his parking area to let the attendant know that he wants his car washed and detailed, hoping that it is not too late. While speaking with the parking attendant, finding out if he has waited too late, someone walks up behind James and taps him on the shoulder. James turns around, and there to his surprise is Miss Jennifer Holt.

"Hello, stranger, I guess I should call you stranger. I have not seen or heard from you. What did you do, destroy my number?"

"It is difficult to explain."

Jennifer jokingly says, "I know, you are a celebrity now. With all of the television coverage you have been receiving lately."

"Trust me, that was not what I wanted."

"You know, we had a pack, call if you are in need. I guess you never did need."

"I can say the same for you. What brings you in our neck of the woods?"

"You mean the high-rent district, don't you?"

"I was in the neighborhood doing a deposition, and I decided to park in this lot, hoping to run into you."

James, smiling, says. "You know, it is nice to see you have not lost any of your sex appeal."

"Likewise, you are looking better than ever. Time has been very kind to you. Oh, I won't keep you. I have to be going. The clock is calling me. You take care. We must do lunch sometimes for old times' sakes."

"I will hold you to it."

The parking attendant talks to James. "Mr. Lackey, we will have your car looking better than ever for you. What time do you want to pick it up?"

"I plan to leave around five thirty."

"Five thirty it is. See you then." James returns to his office.

—ww—

Now that James has returned to his office, he is thinking, *What have I just done? I invited another woman for lunch and she accepted. I will just have to let her know that my life is complete now. That is if she ever calls—*

Mary rings James to let him know that he has a phone call from a representative of the police department. "Something about an auto accident some time ago where a person was shot and you gave the person first aid. The officer tells me that you saved his life."

James replies, "Yes, I do remember that. He called me to set up a meeting here at the office. I had first thought they had forgotten me. I tried to find out more about the wounded person. I even tried calling him, but I was never able to find out anything. Maybe now I can find how this guy is doing."

Mary tells James that she believes the wounded person and his attorney are there and would like to speak with him.

James says, "I thought you said police department."

"I did say police department, and the nice policeman does want to speak with you about the same accident. He is on the phone and wants to speak with you."

"Have the attorney and his client wait for me in the small conference room. I will be with them as soon as I complete the phone call with my friend Mr. Police Officer." He smiles. While speaking with the police officer on the phone, James finds out that an arrest was made in the case some time ago. The police officer tells James that the prosecutor's office would like to speak with him as soon as it is possible and the phone call is to finalize that meeting. The prosecution rep on the line confirms to James that he is wanted as a witness. They want to find out just what James was able to see that night, or if he was able to observe anything unusual taking place before, during, or after the car ran off the road that night. James agrees to meet with the prosecutor and speak the truth about everything he observed that night. The officer tells James that the victim that night is not a model citizen. He has a long history of criminal activity in his background. They suspect this was a retaliation shooting.

James is speechless. He just says, "Anything that I can provide that can help bring closure to this incident, you can count on me." James finally hangs up the phone from the police office by committing to meet with the prosecutor's office. Now he thinks, *Maybe this was a gangland-style murder attempt. I did not see a crime take place. I only observed the victim driving erratically and driving over the small embankment. This is turning out to be a very interesting to me, especially since I have the victim and his attorney waiting to speak with me.*

James immediately joins the attorney and his client in the conference room. The attorney just so happens to be an attorney that James recognizes as always involved in high-profile cases, a reputation for being very expensive to retain, specializing in high-profile criminal cases by the name of Joe Jackson. James introduces himself to Attorney Jackson, and in return, the attorney introduces himself to James. He also recognizes James and reminds him of such. Attorney Jackson now introduces James to his client Mr. Thomas Steiner, who immediately recognizes James. It seems that James's daughter Debbie is a former cheerleader for the same high school that Mr. Steiner attended. Mr. Steiner also recognizes James as a prominent attorney and from the recent media coverage of James's involvement with Karen Campbell. The meeting gets started. They all take a seat at the table.

Attorney Jackson leads of the meeting by telling James, "Even though my client is a victim in this case and a person is being tried for attempted murder against him, the prosecution is also claiming an illegal activity that my client was having that night. The perpetrator of the crime will go to jail for attempted murder, but now the prosecution is claiming that it was a revenge crime against my client, and my client was in the process of committing a crime at the time the shooting took place. They want to prosecute my client for multiple crimes taking place that night when he was shot multiple times. Our question is, did you observe anything unusual happening to or in Tom's car?"

James replies, "To be honest with you, counselor, I did not see anything but an injured man that I attempted to help until the paramedics arrived and took over the care. I did see the car being driven erratically. I was interviewed that same evening by the police about what I had seen. They have my story, and my story did not include information about my seeing anything unusual taking place, I told the police that night I did not observe anything unusual happening that night other than a wounded man that I found out have been shot after I began giving him first aid.

Attorney Jackson says, "You know you were instrumental in possibly saving Mr. Steiner's life."

"I was only doing what any other red-blooded citizen would have done."

Mr. Steiner says, "I want to thank you, Mr. Lackey."

"You are welcome!"

Attorney Jackson says, "We really just wanted to meet you, touch base with you, and see if there is any possible help that we could get from you. We want to thank you for taking the time out of your schedule to meet with us at this late time of the day."

Thomas Steiner adds, "I want to thank you also, Mr. Lackey. You saved my life."

"Both of you are welcome. Good luck with the prosecutor and good luck with this case. I will be here if you need me."

Attorney Jackson says, "We will keep that in mind."

James says, "I have to be up front with you and let you know that the phone call I was receiving when you guys arrived was from law enforcement, a representative of the prosecutor's office. I will be meeting with the prosecution soon."

Attorney Jackson says. "Well we knew they would have interest in speaking with you. We just want you to tell the truth."

"That is all I can do." The two men thank James and excuse themselves.

—◊—

James returns from the conference room to his office. It is now getting late in the day, Most os the office staff is preparing to leave for the day. James places a call to see it his car will be ready as promised and is told that his car will be ready on time. James is now placing a call to Claudette to see it she has any plans this evening. Claudette tells James that she promised her daughter Peggy that she would go shopping with her to help her decide on the purchase of a nice dress for the wedding.

James says, "I understand you guys are going shopping. Have fun!"

"I hope so. Peggy really takes her time. When I go shopping with Peggy, I know I have to be patient."

"You guys have fun and be good while doing do."

"We are always good!" James and Claudette are humorously saying good-bye. James now realizes that it will be dinner alone tonight, maybe pick up some take-out, watch a little TV, and off to bed.

James completes his day in the office and ends up in the neighborhood bar that is the hangout for many of the office staffs in and around the neighborhood. James realizes that there are a few employees from his office present. James soon finds out that also present is Attorney Joe Jackson and his client Thomas Steiner. Attorney Jackson observes James entering the bar and approached him with an offer to allow him to buy James a drink. James in courteous to his fellow attorney but is not interested in socializing with him, not even for a friendly drink. James apologizes for not being able to share a drink with them and tells the attorney that he is scheduled to meet someone there, maybe next time. James recognizes the face of a young attorney from his office, approaches him, and begins a conversation. Attorney Jackson does not let James's reason for not having a drink with him and his client prevent him from continually approaching James to have a drink with the two of them. James continually excused himself and tells the attorney that he does not have the time to become involved in much dialogue with him. Finally, James just excuses himself and heads for home without a drink or take-out.

A few days later, it is a Saturday morning. James, Grant, Patty, and Eugene are enjoying a golf outing at the members-only gold course where James is a member and the golf course that James and Sam played their last round of golf together. The foursome is finishing up their round of golf, and it seems that Patty has been the better golfer once again. Her uncle and two brothers are now challenging each other to find out just who is the loser on this final hole between the three of them. The loser pays for all snacks and drinks. After the completion of this round of golf, they all head for the clubhouse and is seated having some good conversation, bragging about their round of golf and how well Patty was playing. The tall tales about the missed putts, the drive out of bound, mostly the fact that Patty beat all of them. Gene says she beats her husband too. He won't even play with her. Everyone is jovial, and James is happy that he could spend this day with his brother's family, playing the game that he and his brother use to spend so much time playing when they were growing up. This has been a most relaxing day for James and his two nephews and niece. James feels that maybe this is the best kind of therapy to overcome the lost of his brother. He only wishes that Carol and Mary could enjoy this kind of camaraderie. As the time passes and there is not very many more exaggerations left, now is the time for everyone to start preparing to leave for home after paying their check. Gene suggests that they should do this again and more often and next time invite some other members of the family. "Maybe we can get enough of us Lackeys together for two foursomes. Maybe even my brother-in-law who won't play with his wife might join us."

Grant says, "Let's make sure they are in the same foursome." They're all laughing at each other's bad jokes, because this has been a good day for all. They get into their cars and head for home.

—∞—

James did not leave immediately. He remains in the parking lot, putting his golf clubs into his car as he instead decides to place a phone call to Claudette just before starting his car to suggest that the two of them go out for a nice dinner tonight and celebrate. Claudette wants to know what will be celebrating. James tells Claudette that they will be celebrating maybe their most enjoyable life together.

Claudette, laughing, says, "Our most enjoyable life together!"

"Yes, out enjoyable life together. We have not always known each other, so now let's celebrate our life, as we know it."

"I will be there at six, ready or not."

"I will be ready."

James says, "Until six." He starts up his car and heads for home. James decides to take the scenic route home along the waterfront where people are out strolling, surfing, and enjoying the beach. James likes this drive. He remembers taking this drive with Margie on many occasions. This has been a very nice day weather-wise, and James feels that he must enjoy it as much as possible as he drives, also thinking about as many nice things that has taken place in his life as he can. James feels that with all of the setbacks that have happened in his life recently, life has been very good to him. He has been blessed. His law practice is a success. He has a wonderful family that cares for him, a good woman that loves him, and his brother had a wonderful wife and family, plus a life that had purpose. He will always miss him, but he is going to live his life. "I will just prepare myself for an enjoyable evening with Claudette."

—∭—

James wake the following morning at home in bed with Claudette with a big smile on his face.

Claudette looks over at James now that he is awake, saying, "Last night was a good night." With a big smile on her face and looking in James's eyes, she shares, "When I was a young woman, people use to tell me that men and women our age forgot about making real passionate love, or just having sex period, but I am here to tell the world that it is not true. Sex is not only good but special at this age, and last night was even better. What you got, I don't want to lose."

James reaches over and puts his arm around Claudette and says, "You want some more?"

Claudette says, "What do you think?"

James rolls over on Claudette as the two of them are embracing and kissing, raising up from the kiss, saying, "I got you now."

Claudette hugs him back and says, "You are just where you want to be." Time passes an finally Claudette says in a joyful tone, "We had better get up from here. We will have to get dressed for church and hope we can be forgiven for a night of lovemaking." James says the next chapter just might include more of what we did not finish. The two of them jump out of bed to get dressed because she does not have a change of clothes that she can wear to church. James hurries into the shower and quickly gets dressed.

—m—

Church is now over, and James and Claudette are driving along the street remembering that they have not eaten breakfast. James asks Claudette if she would like to have a late breakfast or brunch. Claudette responds, "I would like to go somewhere that we can sit and eat. I do not care if it is breakfast food or not." James and Claudette agree on a place to eat, and as they drive to the location, James is thinking, *If me and Claudette are living together as husband and wife, problem would be solved on a Sunday morning before church and after a night of lovemaking, but is this what Claudette wants?* James decides to ask Claudette what she would think about the two of them living together.

Claudette looking at James is startled. "James Lackey! What would my kids say or what would your kids say?"

"Not like that. I mean if we are husband and wife."

Claudette, smiling, says, "Would you want to marry me? I mean, I am a woman pass sixty years old. I mean pass sixty."

"We are both pass sixty and getting no younger. At least we would have companionship in our old age."

"You know I would marry you. Let's pass this by our committee of children who you already know think they know best for us." James looks at Claudette with a smile of happiness on his face.

"We can pass it by them but the final decision is yours and mine." Claudette just looks at James and smiles as they are arriving at the location to eat.

—⟐—

The following morning, which is a Monday morning, James is busy working in his office but cannot get his mind of the idea of his and Claudette's conversation about marriage, so he places a call to Claudette. Claudette answers the phone. "Hello?" James says hello as Claudette says, "What is wrong? You changed your mind?" She laughingly says, "It is too late to change your mind now."

James says, "Nothing like that. I was calling to say why don't you and I go shopping this evening for a ring. You know, an engagement ring, telling our family and friends that we are getting married, which I hope will be soon. I can be over to pick you up just as soon as I get off from here."

"I guess you are really serious about wanting to marry me. I had better start preparing myself to be Mrs. James Lackey. What time would you want to go shopping?"

"I would be out of here about six and can pick you up around six thirty."

Claudette is very happy as she agrees with James and says, "I will be ready."

James is very happy, calls his assistant Mary into his office, and says "Mary, I am not supposed to tell anybody and you had better not repeat this, but I am getting married. Claudette agreed to marry me."

Mary looks at James and says, "I am very happy for you." She then runs over and gives James a hug. "I won't tell anybody! Did you guys set a date?"

James says, "Not yet, but I hope it will be soon."

Mary says, "Isn't Mrs. Claudette's son Brad getting married soon?"

"Yes, they already have a date, place, and time all picked out. They should be mailing out invitations any day now. I first gave thought to a double ceremony, but I wouldn't want to spoil their big day. Anyway, I think Claudette and I deserve our own special day with our friends and our family."

"I will have to start helping you with your guest list. I can also help Mrs. Claudette if she needs help."

"I am sure she will. I will tell her that she can depend on you."

―⚭―

James is now receiving a phone call directly on his cell phone. He answers and it is Jennifer Holt. "Hello, remember me? I am the struggling attorney that you use to run into every so often and I do mean run into." She starts laughing.

James replied, "Yes, I do remember you with pleasure."

"If you remember, I have a lunch date promised."

"I do seem to remember something like that."

"When can I collect your debt?"

"Maybe tomorrow. I am available for lunch."

"I can meet you around twelve thirty."

"I will have a reservation for two at the little place we first had a meal. It seems that they all know you there."

"That is a date."

Now James is thinking, *I am a real hypocrite. I have just made a date with another woman immediately after making an appointment to go shopping for a ring with the woman I truly do love. I must not go through with that lunch date.*

―⚭―

Later that evening, James and Claudette are shopping form store to store for a ring. James is truly happy to do so, but he is also feeling guilty for accepting a lunch date with Jennifer.

It is not the right thing to do. It is not fair to Jennifer who is only out to have a little fun, and it really is not fair to Claudette, a wonderful woman that is in love with him. The sex as James remembers with Jennifer is very good with no strings attached. James is thinking, *Maybe one more time. No one will know but Jennifer and I.*

Claudette is so vibrant and smiling with so much happiness showing in her face. James does not want to change what he is seeing in Claudette. Claudette has finally found the ring that she just loves after trying it on.

Claudette says, "I don't want to take it off. Don't you just love it, honey?"

"It looks good on your finger. Let us have her wrap this one. Better still, why don't you just wear it home?"

Claudette hugs James and tells the salesperson, "I think we are taking this one. Give the box to me. I am wearing it home." Claudette and James purchase the ring that reminds Claudette that happiness is always possible. After paying for the ring, they leave the jewelry store very animated. Claudette is really happy, but James is not happy, having mixed feeling knowing that he is not being totally faithful to Claudette.

Following morning, James sits in his office knowing that if he goes through with his lunch date with Jennifer, he is being unfaithful to Claudette, because he knows that a date with Jennifer has always ended up in bed. As the time grows near, James is now nervous about what can happen. Finally James is leaving for his lunch date determined that it is only a lunch and nothing else. James arrived at the restaurant and finds out that Jennifer is running a little late. James chooses to be seated and wait. He is waiting and is even more nervous. Finally,

Jennifer approaches his table with a distinguished-looking young man about the same age as Jennifer. After all of the usual hellos, Jennifer introduces the young man as Alexander Melvin to James as her fiancé. James stands for the two of them to seat themselves, is happily surprised, and shakes the young man's hand.

Jennifer says. "Alex and I have known each other for many years. We met in law school. Yes, he is an attorney just like you and I. Our lives separated for a few years until we met again recently working as adversaries on a case. The rest led us to where we are today, and we plan to be married soon. We want to invite you and your guest to our wedding, so look for the invite."

"I want to congratulate you guys. I am so happy for you. I am getting married also." The three of them let out a big laugh, as they are getting ready to order lunch.

James is now back at work. "Whew! That was a close one. I will never get myself into that kind of trouble again. Let me call Claudette so I can reassure myself that I am still happily engaged." James is not able to find Claudette at home. Claudette is keeping a promise to Brad by attending an afternoon musical session in a musical rehearsing studio, watching Brad and Diana's musical group, rehearsing music that Brad and Diana are planning to perform as a surprise to James at his and Claudette's wedding. James has often been told but never seen or heard any of Brad and Diana's music performances.

Getting the correct mindset for their wedding, James exudes much happiness and is staying busy at home and around the office. Preparing for his marriage to Claudette is a little crazy these days for James, and as James tells it, it all revolves around staying in touch with reality and a lot of craziness.

—w—

James and Claudette are preparing to host an all-inclusive family gathering at Claudette's house for next Sunday, which will be a surprise announcement of their wedding plans. This surprise announcement for their wedding plans will be for a small group of family, a few select friends, and a few colloquies. This surprise is very important to both James and Claudette. They are not telling anyone the reason for this gathering.

—w—

On the day of the wedding proposal announcement, James and Claudette are preparing themselves for the arrival of their family. Claudette is not feeling well. She is experiencing pain and discomfort in her joints due to her rheumatoid arthritis. Claudette does not want to alarm James or the family about her pain but knows that she cannot keep it to herself, so she tells James about her pain. James asks Claudette is there is anything that he can do to make things more comfortable for her. Claudette says to James, "I have taken a pain pill, which is medication that I take in accordance with her doctor's recommendation. I am hoping that it will provide some relief. You know, we had better get ready before the gang arrives."

James looks at Claudette with a slight smile and gives her a hug. "I guess you are right, but if you are having any kind of problems, you must tell me. I can handle what needs to be done to get ready, so you take it easy."

Claudette with a big smile tells James, "Now you know why I love you and is happy to marry you. You are so thoughtful and kind." James and Claudette continue to prepare for the arrival of all their guests.

Claudette is not feeling well, but her discomfort is now tolerable. The families begin to arrive and are surprised to fine the house set up in such a festive and party-looking atmosphere. There are plenty of food and refreshments to be served, with lively music. It is not long before all of the two families expected seem to be present. Much fun, food, and drink are being consumed. There is even a little dancing. James walks up and pretends to have a microphone and asks for everyone's attention, "Can I have your attention?" the music stops, and all of the attention is focused on James and Claudette, except for a couple of the young grandchildren who want to keep playing.

James says, "We called all if you here tonight because we have an announcement to make and we want to share it with the people in our lived that mean the most to the two of us." Claudette is nodding approval of what James is saying. "You all know Claudette and I have been friends for a while now, and as a matter of fact, we have grown rather fond of each other." They hug. "What I am saying, we, two senior tax-paying Americans pass sixty years old, have found love again. I know that you must be saying, 'How can this be happening?' Debbie and Pam are saying, 'What about Mom?' In the case of Pearce, Peggy, and Brad, you are probably asking the same question about your dad."

Brad raises his hand for attention and speaks up, "I am not saying anything. I just want my mom to be happy. She is getting old, you know." Laughter erupts/ "You make my mom happy, and I remember how miserable she was living with me, after my accident." Laughter erupts again. "So I am going to refer to you as Dad and pretend I'm happy."

Debbie, remembering how Claudette has been there for her, the same as if though Claudette is her mother during her cancer fight, says, "We'll I guess it is no secret to everybody what my reactions were when I first found out about the two of you together." The laughter continues. "Now my voice is silent"—pointing to Claudette–"Mom."

Pam says, "The day when your voice is silent id the day we will all be saying, 'RIP, Debbie,'" Laughter erupts.

Debbie, pointing to Pam, says, "I can do without comments from peanut gallery."

Brad, with a bit of smile as he attempts to be humorous, says, "I guess you are over the biggest two disasters and stumbling blocks in these two families. Then you get Deb and me to join hands as family, minus opposition under the new family tent." Unanimous approval of this new potential family proposal by all present is now being articulated by all five of James and Claudette's children following Brad and Debbie's approval.

James, showing happiness and laughter, says, "Before all of the commentary that interrupted my speech, I did not get to the good part. This is an announcement that we are engaged and plan to be married real soon." Immediate joy overcomes the room. Everyone is happy and begins to propose a toast to James and Claudette, which has lasted for a few minutes. Peggy runs up and gives James a hug. The same display of affection is now on display with all of their children and grandchildren. Once all of the toasting is over, James and Claudette tell everyone their wedding plans, date and honeymoon plans.

Brad, hugging Diana, says, "You know, we, Diana and I, have wedding plans also. Maybe a double wedding could be the word of the day. That is if you guys won't mind delaying your wedding plans a bit. You know the dates are now that far apart."

"Well, Claudette and I figure that is you guys' special day and we don't want to get in the way of your wedding because you will find out sometime in the future just how special your wedding day is."

Claudette nods in agreement and says, "After all, this will be our special day too, and we don't want to share or delay it."

James says, "You know, we gave thought to the possibility of a double wedding, but decided against it."

Pearce says, "Well we will be celebrating twice, for twice as much fun." The family party continues. Everyone is enjoying themselves and in some cases meeting each other for the first time.

—⟨w⟩—

Sunday afternoon, James is kneeling at Margie's gravesite speaking to Margie and telling Margie's grave that he will be getting married soon and his visits to her gravesite will be discontinued out of respect for Claudette. James is also telling Margie's grave how happy he feels whenever he is with Claudette and that Debbie and Pam have accepted Claudette in their lives and are happy for him. Now they won't have to worry about him being alone anymore. "Between Pam, Debbie and Claudette's three children, there will be plenty concerned family to look after me. Rest in peace, honey!"

—⚏—

The following evening, James and Claudette are together at their favorite restaurant having dinner celebrating and discussing how pleased they are that their wedding plans meet with unanimous approval of all of their children and is a go. All of a sudden, Claudette is feeling unbearable pain and joint discomfort, so much so that she is now going to faint, eventually passing out. James is in a panic trying to get her some help, calling the paramedics, calling every number that he thinks might be able to provide help for Claudette. James is thinking heart attack, asking if there is anyone in the restaurant that has some medical experience. A woman rushes over to James announcing that she is a doctor. She begin an attempt to diagnose the problem and providing help for Claudette. A short time later, the paramedics arrives and began to try to revive Claudette with the help of the doctor. Claudette is rushed off to the emergency ward at the hospital for medical attention where she is able to speak after a short time, telling the doctor, "O am hurting everywhere, and I have a very bad headache." James continues his panic state not being able to accompany Claudette to the examining area, trying to call his and her children without all of the phone numbers being accessible to him. James is trying to notify all of them of Claudette's condition which he does not know. James is also frustrated that the doctor in charge cannot tell him anything about what caused Claudette to be suffering or what is wrong with her. After a brief period, the doctor tells James that Claudette is now coherent and he can visit with her. The doctor tells James that Claudette is asking for him. Not too much time passes and Claudette's children along with his children are beginning to arrive. They all are asking questions, without many answers. James has already been cleared for entrance to the emergency area where Claudette is being attended to. As James enters the treatment area, he is happy to see Claudette is awake. Claudette recognizes James with a painful smile and says, "This is what you will have to deal with if you marry this old woman."

Jams gazes back at Claudette with a smile. "I just want you to feel better before the wedding."

Claudette says, "You know, as we always say, 'Love is now always easy.' Loving me is proof that the statement is true." The doctor enters the area where Claudette is and explains to James and Claudette that some tests are being run on Claudette. He is not sure why she suffered this reaction, so he would like to have her admitted at least for the night.

"A room is being prepares for her as we speak. The nurse has the room number that she will be admitted to and you can get is from her." Claudette wants to know if any of her children has been notified, and James assures her that he has notified them himself.

The nurse tells Claudette that several people had arrived and would like to see her, but maybe they should wait and see her once she has been moved to a room. "At that time, you will be able to see more than one of them at a time."

Claudette looks up at James and says, "That is probably best. I agree. Tell them that I am okay and hope to see them soon."

The nurse says, "I will!"

Some time later, Claudette is finally in the room that she will be for the remainder of the night. After a period of time, Claudette is feeling much better and is enjoying her visits from her family. She is now able to have more than one person visit at a time. All three of her children and in-laws are able to visit with her. Pam and Debbie are also able to visit with her. The problem that Claudette is having now is that she never did get to eat the meal that was delivered to their table at the restaurant and is very hungry. Claudette is asking for food at this late hour, long after the hospital has completed service dinner. The nurse on duty promises Claudette that she will arrange for a meal to be delivered to Claudette, even if she has to prepare it herself. Later that evening, the doctor from the hospital emergency area visits Claudette's room and explains to Claudette and her family that Claudette will be okay. She has a reaction from one of the medications that was prescribed to her. Claudette is allergic to a medication that has been identified. There will have to be a change in her medications. Claudette commences to explain her recent rheumatoid arthritis diagnosis to the doctor. Everyone is relieved to know that there is nothing seriously wrong with Claudette, and her problem can be solved with a change in a medication. The doctor informed Claudette that she will more than likely be going home tomorrow after it is confirmed that her condition is just a reaction. Claudette is happy to hear that all is well and she can go home. The entire family is happy with the news.

Brad tells all, "I will pick up mother up from the hospital whatever time of the day she will be released. That is the least I can do with all she did for me during my time of need." No one argues with him and agrees to have Brad take Claudette home from the hospital.

Claudette says, "We will have to mail those wedding invitations out immediately. I hope we have our guest list in order."

James tells Claudette that his assistant Mary Winfield has offered to help her. "Don't you worry about wedding invitations right now. You just get well. We will think about them after you are better." All agree.

—⚏—

It is early afternoon the following day. Claudette is home from the hospital, feeling a bit busy and excited that the wedding remains on track. Claudette now knows that she has to complete the guest list for the wedding, pick up the invitations, and prepare them to be mailed. Claudette's doorbell rings. She opens the door, and standing there as expected is her daughter Peggy.

Peggy says, "Hi, Mom, are you ready to go shopping?"

Claudette responds, "As ready as I will ever be. Come on in while I put my shoes on." As Claudette puts her shoes on to go shopping, Peggy is asking her is she is feeling okay.

Claudette says, "I am feeling fine, a lot better than last evening. You don't know it but I was not an early riser this morning. I was still confined to that hospital bed, waiting to be released. Brad was there on time. I am now ready. Let's go shopping, "The two of them leave the house and head for Peggy's car.

—⚏—

As the afternoon begins to wind down, James is arriving at his home golf course's driving range to hit a few golf balls so he can get rid of some tension that has been strolling up inside of him. Upon James's arrival and his securing a couple of buckets of golf ball, he immediately notices that Karen Campbell is busy hitting golf balls on the driving range. James returns to the clubhouse to find out if anyone could answer the question of the presence of Karen Campbell. After some time and many questions, James is not able to locate anyone that could explain to him the presence of Karen or how she is able to gain entrance to the private establishment. James does not want to be seen by Karen Campbell and decides to remain inside of the clubhouse, hoping Karen would finish and leave, but once Karen has completed hitting as many golf ball as she wanted, she comes inside of the clubhouse, located a table, and orders a drink. Karen appears as if though she has plans to sit for a while. James finally decides to depart for home, wondering how and why Karen is at his home golf course. There must be some answers some place, and he plans to find the underlying cause of this mystery.

The following day, James is still wondering about the presence of Karen at the golf course, which is a well-known hangout of his. James begins to find out about the restraining order that is in place. Maybe once again, Karen is in violation of the restraining order. James is also thinking about the help that Karen is in need of and maybe the right thing for him to do is to find out about her much-needed help. James immediately finds out that Karen is missing from the house that she has been living and receiving some much-needed help, but has been located and returned to this unsecured location. James is promised that there is some medium lockup at this facility and Karen is going to be immediately placed in a secure area. James does not feel that this will solve the problem but will have to live with it.

Wedding day, James is dressed for his wedding, wondering what Claudette is wearing. James is now meeting in the pastor's office with Pastor Bledsoe, with him in addition to Pastor Bledsoe is his older brother's son, Eugene Lackey, who will be standing as James's best man. James is nervous, and it really is evident in James's demeanor. Eugene is trying to calm his uncle down with a few of his late dad's bad jokes. It is getting a laugh from James.

—∾—

Claudette is dressed in little early, just sitting and waiting to be escorted down the aisle by her oldest son Pearce. Final touches on Claudette's makeup and hair are being taken care of. She is wondering about James and his demeanor.

Claudette's daughter Peggy enters the area, saying, "Are you ready, Mama? You don't want to back out now I hope, but if you do, your time is running out."

Claudette jokingly says, "I'm ready, I am as ready as will ever be. If I back out now and can't get another one, you and Jim will have to provide me with a room because I will be moving in with you guys."

—∾—

Pastor Bledsoe enters the room to inform James that the time has arrived. They must now join the rest of the party out front. James and Eugene are preparing to take their places in the church along with the rest of the groomsmen. As they arrive and take their proper place, the music begins to play, and the bridesmaids begin their entrance to join them. Upon the completion of the entrance of bridesmaids, the music stops and the music for Claudette's entrance begins. The doors open and Claudette and Pearce appears. They begin their walk. James turns to view Claudette and Pearce, and to his dismay, there is Karen Campbell sitting in the middle of the audience staring at him. James is once again wondering how is Karen able to always be present wherever he is. James decides not to let Karen's presence affect him and focus all of his attention on Claudette and how wonderful she looks.

—⚬—

Claudette and Pearce arrive at the podium. Pastor Bledsoe proceeds with the ceremony. James looks into Claudette's eyes and says softly to Claudette, "You look wonderful. I am a very lucky man."

Claudette, smiling, says, "I am the lucky one." The two of them soon become so involved in their own dialogue that they fail to hear Pastor Bledsoe reciting the marriage and asking them to commence with their vows.

The guest are laughing at the lack of attention James and Claudette are paying to Pastor Bledsoe and how they seem to only be interested in each other. Pastor Bledsoe looks a little stunned as he says jokingly, "Are we having a marriage ceremony here, or is this just a conversation between you two that does not include any of the rest of us?"

James jokingly says to Claudette, "I think we had better get on with this. Somebody is getting a little testy, and you know we have been messing around long enough."

Claudette, smiling, says, "Why not?"

Pastor Bledsoe jokingly says, "So glad we are all finally back on the same page. Thanks again for you guys' attention. We were beginning to think you are not interested in what I have to say."

Pastor Bledsoe continues with the ceremonies. Once he reaches to the point if there is anyone that objects with the marriage to let them speak, Karen Campbell interrupts the ceremonies by standing and saying, "I object to this charade!" Karen rushes to the podium, grabs Claudette by her arm, pushes Claudette to the floor, and attempts to grab James's arm. The scene becomes chaotic.

Brad rushes over and grabs Karen and starts yelling, "Call the police. Call the police." He throws Karen to the floor and refuses to let her loose. This chaotic situation continues for some time until finally two police officers come running into the church and take custody of Karen Campbell.

They announce to Karen. "We are going to have to take you in." The officers request from Pastor Bledsoe that they will want to know the details of this suspected disturbance. The wedding continues to be held up until the officers completes their brief questions period with Pastor Bledsoe, James, Claudette, and Brad. The officers announce that they will need a complete list of names present there today, because maybe they just might want to speak with other people present. "We hope all has signed the guest list, but if not, please sign it after the ceremony."

This period of investigation will last as short time s possible as the officer's could make it, knowing that a wedding is taking place. Finally, calm is restored, and Karen is now being taken away. Pastor Bledsoe is very calm. Claudette's dress is a bit out of shape and torn. She looks confused. James starts apologizing to the guest and explaining Karen's problems as he understands them. "You might be familiar with media reports of Karen stalking me."

Claudette is thinking, *How can this wedding continue now that my dress is messed up and torn?*"

James asks Claudette, "Are you okay? I see your dress is a little messed up, but not that bad, I say let's go with it. What are your wishes?"

"I am fine now. Just wondering how do I look."

"You look just beautiful. Your dress now has character, and I think we should continue."

"Well if you say continue, let us continue."

James winks at Claudette and says, "I love you!"

Pastor Bledsoe speaks softly to James and Claudette, "We can proceed now, and that is if you people want to continue."

James says, "Let's get this over with. We are not waiting another minute longer!"

Pastor Bledsoe says, "I hear you." He continues with the ceremony. The ceremony is over. The guest are exiting the church in a festive mood, cheering the newly weds as they exit the church to enter the limo to be driven away.

One year has passed, James and Claudette are very happily married. James continued to work in his law practice and is much calmer as a happily married man. Claudette is keeping herself busy as she becomes much more involved in her charities and is also back at work on a part-time basis for the accounting firm that her late husband and she built. She spends time with all of her and James's Children. Her rheumatoid arthritis is under control. James and Claudette are not living in a new home. Debbie's cancer is in remission, and Brad and Diana are newly weds. Expecting their first child. At the same time, their music careers are beginning to show signs of some success.

Karen Campbell remains in the custody of the state confined to an institution that requires her to be locked up indefinitely. There is hope that this institution can provide her with the treatment that maybe one day can cure her. Karen seems to be finally enjoying herself, by being very active every day, playing games and making friends, with a daily job assignment in the institutions reception area, which allows for her to meet new people as they visit their loved ones. Maybe or hopefully, she has forgotten all about James Earl Lackey.